Student of Babel

Davin Hall

Davin Hall
Greensboro, North Carolina
www.davinhall.com

Print ISBN: 979-8-9864541-0-8
eBook ISBN: 979-8-9864541-1-5

This is a work of fiction. Any similarities between characters and situations to places or persons living or dead is entirely coincidental.

First Edition

to the unfathomable chaos that brings us together

Student of Babel

ONE

THE PLAGIARIST

The school sat by the edge of a sea. It was in a bit of a hollow, presumably an area that had been underwater many cycles ago, but was now home to the school. It had stood there for a long time. No one knew quite how long. A red dusty plain, scattered with rocks, stretched out for some distance before coming to an abrupt end at a ridge that drew a semi-circle around the hollow. Atop the ridge, large boulders could be seen from the school, but that was all.

I wish I could tell you how long the school had been there.

Footsteps padded softly in the hall. The two pairs of gray sandals were identical, apart from size; the larger belonging to a man, the smaller to a boy no more than twelve. They walked purposefully, but not so fast for the boy to have to hurry.

As they walked, they passed closed doors on their right and small windows set into large, pale red bricks on their left. Light glowed from the ceiling and came gently through the tinted windows.

The boy's eyes constantly roamed across the hall. He identified each door individually, by the cracks in the paint, the chips in the door frame. The entire ceiling glowed but he saw the thin spider web of filaments criss-crossing that shone with white light. Each window told a different story, looking out on a slightly different patch of the dusty yard than its neighbor. The door at the end of the hall was frightening. He'd only been through it a few times before. The hallway was long, but each step was unique, a section of the boy's world that was not like any other.

The man walked down the same hallway but he recognized the doors on their order, their relation to one another. The ceiling glowed uniformly and the windows all looked out on the same view. The door at the end of the hall was one he had passed through many times and it held no fear for him. Only a curiosity about what was to be done and how the boy had managed the crime.

They walked side-by-side in silence. Though they were in the same building, the same hallway, each walked in his own world, far distant from the other.

When they arrived at the oak-like door at the end, the man opened it without hesitating, stepping easily into the room. The boy followed behind, feeling his heart beat louder in his constricting chest. He wiped his palms on his beige habit, not noticing the damp mark left behind.

The Principal's office was large, extending off to the right from the door. Heavy navy curtains hung by the windows, tied back to let the natural light in. The floor was still tile but with several thick rugs asymmetrically placed. Along the inside wall, bookcases stretched from floor to ceiling, running the length of the entire wall. A rolling ladder sat about halfway down and a large armchair was in the corner, flanked by windows. At the end of the room was a desk where a small, white-haired man was sitting. Three chairs were in front of the desk for visitors.

The boy walked after the man toward the desk, being careful not to trip on a corner of a rug. His world shrank to the size of the room and then further still until it was just a small bubble encapsulating the boy and the Principal.

"Thank you, Arden," the white-haired man said, softly. "Might you observe from the reading chair?" He gestured politely at the armchair in the corner. The man retreated.

The boy stood very still.

A smile flickered over the Principal's face. "Might you sit down for me?" He gestured gracefully again, this time at the chair closest to the boy.

The boy sat, quickly. He looked down at his hands, then out the window, then behind him at the man just sitting down in the armchair, then a flash at the Principal before returning his gaze to his lap.

The Principal's gray eyes peered down at the boy.

"Do you understand why you're here, my lad?" the Principal asked.

His voice was always that way, soft, quiet. Sometimes during an assembly, the boy and his friends could barely hear him. They'd lean forward, straining to catch every syllable, asking each neighbor if they'd made it out. There was a rumor that long ago an older Principal had been a great angry man, who shouted and raged all the time, and everyone was terribly frightened. But it was just a rumor and didn't make any sense anyway. No one here could remember anyone like that. The boy imagined this Principal yelling and throwing books at students and teachers, and had to stifle a giggle.

"Yes, sir," he said, solemnly.

"Oh?" the Principal raised his eyebrows and leaned back. "Why is it then?"

There was a silence. The boy hadn't expected that. He merely didn't want to tell the Principal 'no'. The silence lengthened and the man in the chair stirred, clearing his throat quietly.

"Yes?" the Principal said.

The boy's eyes shifted left to right, and back. Something occurred to him. The last thing he'd written had been sent to the Principal. Pency had told him. He looked up. "You liked my story?"

An amused snort came from the corner. The Principal

blinked, but smiled.

"I did like your story," the Principal said. "But I'm afraid that's not the whole reason you're here."

"Oh," the boy was dejected.

"It was a very excellent story," the Principal said quickly. "It is a very excellent story," he corrected his tense. The boy looked up again.

"Thank you, sir."

"May I ask..." the Principal paused, and looked at the ceiling. The boy waited.

"It's Geoffrey," the boy said, politely.

"What?" the Principal looked at the boy again, a confused look on his face.

"My name? It's Geoffrey. I thought..." the boy hesitated. "You'd forgotten. I was trying to help."

The Principal smiled. "No, my lad. Geoffrey. I know your name."

"Oh," the boy was embarrassed.

The Principal cocked his head to the side to look down at Arden in the chair, who was biting his lip. He returned his attention to the boy.

"May I ask where you came up with the idea for your story?"

"Oh," the boy said again. "I dunno, sir. I was just writing."

"Yes," the Principal leaned forward and brought his hands together on the top of his desk. "Ah, what inspired you to write a vampiric story?"

The Principal's voice was casual but the boy was worried. Why was he asking about this story? Had he done something wrong?

"I..." the boy said. "I've been reading some similar books. From the time period. Gothic horror? And I thought I would try to do something similar." He frowned. "Was that wrong?"

"No, no, no, no, no, my lad," the Principal said, hurriedly.

"I'd just like to know more about the good decisions you made."

"Oh," the boy smiled.

"The, ah, names. The people and the places. Did you come up with those on your own?"

"Mostly," the boy said, leaning back. Now he understood. This was a professional conversation between two experienced writers. His story had catapulted him onto the same level as the masters. It was about time. "I had read about some of the named places, but the characters I came up with," the boy said.

"Mhm," said the Principal. "And had you read Sheridan Le Fanu before?"

The boy paused, confused by the phrasing. "Yes," he said, hesitantly. "I've read Uncle Silas."

"And Carmilla?" asked the Principal.

"Yes," said the boy, still confused.

"You read it?" the Principal asked, peering closely at the boy.

"That's my story," said the boy, more confused.

"Ah," the Principal said. The room was quiet again. The boy looked down, knitting his brow. What on the world was going on here? "Geoffrey," began the Principal. Geoffrey looked up. "Sometimes..." he said, and paused, staring down at his desk. "Sometimes when we try to imitate a previous author or style, we end up doing a little more than that." Geoffrey's forehead crinkled more. "Sometimes we take more than we intended." The Principal raised his head to look at Geoffrey. "Do you understand me, my lad?"

Geoffrey looked back at the Principal. "Yes?" he said.

"And..." the Principal said. "Is that what happened here?"

Geoffrey leaned back slightly, surprised. "No," he said.

"Now, Geoffrey," said the Principal.

"What?" said Geoffrey.

The Principal looked at the boy. Geoffrey felt his forehead crease further and further, and he thought it might crack open. "Geoffrey," said the Principal again. He kept repeating his name. "Were you trying to imitate Carmilla? Or were you simply trying to copy?"

"What are you..." he checked himself; this was the Principal he was talking to, after all. "I don't understand, sir," he said. "What are you referring to? Copy what? My own story?"

The Principal rubbed his hands over his face with some amount of frustration. "No," he said. "Carmilla. By Le Fanu."

"By?" Geoffrey's voice trailed off.

His heart started beating very quickly. Blood rushed into his head, and he felt dizzy. Everything seemed to get blurry around the edges of his vision. It seemed like he couldn't get enough air into his lungs and his hands started tingling. He was afraid of passing out and also desperately wanted to pass out. "Geoffrey?" said the Principal.

"It's a..." he spoke hesitantly. "A real story?" The Principal nodded, while looking gravely at the boy. "It's something somebody wrote already?" The Principal nodded again. "But..." he said. "I never read it before." He saw a muscle twitch in the face of the Principal. "I never read it!" the boy insisted. "And how do you know it's the same story? Maybe it's just close."

"Geoffrey, do not shout."

"I didn't copy!" the boy shouted.

The boy sat in the chair, crying and sniffling. The Principal's face was shot through with discomfort. Arden carefully stood and quietly approached.

"Perhaps," Arden began, and laid a hand gently on the boy's shoulder. The boy leaned into it and grabbed it. Arden knelt down next to the boy, who fell onto him and began sobbing into Arden's habit. "Alright," Arden said, holding the boy. "It's alright, my dear." He and the Principal looked at each other, waiting for the strong emotions to tire themselves out.

For the young boy, the world had ceased to exist, vanished like light during a storm. All his pride at writing something grand had been ripped away, replaced by shame and fear and failure. But most of all, a helplessness at the cruelty of it all. It was not fair. It was not right. And the Principal didn't believe him. He'd be thrown out and starve on the road. Or be eaten by dogs. Or brigands. Or bandits. What was even the difference between a brigand and a bandit? Were they the same? The boy sniffled again, wondering about synonyms for highway robbers. He sighed. "It was just a story I made up," the boy said softly.

There was a quiet moment. The Principal arched his eyebrows at Arden who looked very pained.

"Geoff," Arden leaned back on his heels and looked the boy in the eyes. The boy stared defiantly back. "That's not possible."

"It's certainly the strangest case of plagiarism I've ever seen."

"It's the only case of plagiarism you've ever seen."

"You know what I meant. Besides, that's not true."

"That wasn't plagiarism."

"We didn't know that. We had to convene. Maybe this isn't plagiarism either."

"On Jupiter it isn't."

The two voices bounced gently off the high stone walls, creating a barely perceptible echo. Down the rest of the table, professors hunched over sheaves of paper, trying not to be distracted by the chatter. Arden was bent over his own report, but lifted his eyes to look down the long table to Zeke and Lin at the far end. All the others might be studiously ignoring them, but everyone was probably thinking the same thing.

"Can we please," came an annoyed voice from Nalin. He started over. "I don't think we need the banter right now. Surely it doesn't need to be stressed the importance of this."

Lin raised an eyebrow. "We're not diminishing it, but-"

"The reputation of the school is at stake," interrupted Nalin. "And that of his mentor," he added, looking at Zeke.

Zeke didn't even look up. "Hey," said Lin. "Reputation or no, this is what happened. We have to deal with the fallout now."

"So how did he do it?" Arden asked loudly from the end of the table.

The professors briefly looked up to him, then returned back down. Of the eight faculty members, some peered intently at the report in front of them with confused concern, some looked with a sense of knowing, and some looked simply blank.

At the far end, Lin spoke. "Memorization?"

Across from him, Zeke grunted. "He perfectly memorized a story from a book he's never physically touched? There's not so much as a comma out of place."

"Are we abandoning the if?" This came from the middle of the table, from the oldest voice on the faculty. Arden always felt that if dry hay found a voice, it would speak as bol Win did. The ancient man turned his cloudy green eyes to Arden, expectantly. His skin was so papery, Arden always expected it to tear, in spite of himself. And everything about him was so pale, as though the color had seeped out of him over time. "We're asking how, without asking if?"

Arden shifted in his chair. "I don't think we can reasonably conclude otherwise."

"Ahm," the old man muttered and turned back to his file. "Seems..." the weathered voice trailed away. Everyone waited.

After a moment with nothing more from the ancient

professor, Arden shook his head slightly. "Does anyone have a concern that this is not plagiarism?"

Shaking heads and murmured denials replied. Zeke pursed her lips, but said nothing.

Arden waited an extra moment, then continued. "Good," he said. "Let's..."

"I have concerns," bol Win interrupted. "But go on with you." He waved his hand dismissively.

Arden sighed. "Let's..."

"I'm just an old fool. Don't mind me."

There was no way around it. Arden arched his neck, trying to relieve the tension in his shoulders. "Professor bol Win," he said. "Might you share your concerns, please."

Bol Win nodded. "It's too perfect." There was a pause. The room waited patiently. "I repeat, it is too perfect. Not a character out of place from a book that the boy has never even seen."

"It's too perfect," Lin repeated. "Yes, that's how we know he did it. It couldn't be otherwise. He must have come across the story somehow."

Bol Win slapped the papers in front him with the back of his hand. "Luminescence analysis confirms the book hasn't been touched in three hundred years. None of the micro-genetics attached to it matched the boy, and its chemical signature has never touched him. Unless you doubt Professor Nalin's work?"

Professor Nalin raised her head at the mention.

"Of course not," said Lin. "But-"

"You think the boy got his hands on another copy?" bol Win asked. A murmur of laughter went down the table at the joke.

"It is word for word. Character for character."

"And?"

"It's impossible for it to be anything else. We have

eliminated the impossible, now let's try to find the improbable."

"Oh," bol Win tossed his hands in the air. "That's all we need. A roomful of professors playing at being the world's greatest detective."

"That's enough," Arden said at the other end of the table. "Given the unusual circumstances, we must consider any possibility. Let's focus on the how. That may reveal the if."

Professor Nalin looked up again. "I know this won't be a popular idea, but," she paused. The other professors looked down or away. "Perhaps there was some inspiration at hand. From a higher source."

A series of exhaled frustrations filled the space.

"Are we so arrogant," bol Win's voice lifted over the sighs, quieting them. He paused for what reason Arden could only surmise was dramatic effect. "Are we so arrogant," he repeated, placing a heavy emphasis on arrogant so that it sounded as though he were admonishing his pupils. "...that we would ignore a theory because it runs counter to our pre-existing conceptions? Is that not why we are sitting here now, trying to decipher this mystery?" He stopped, looking out imperiously at his colleagues. Arden could sense half the faculty internally sighing in resignation.

"It's not a testable hypothesis," Zeke said, kindly.

"Perhaps," said bol Win. He turned to Nalin. "Professor? How do you reply?"

Nalin blinked several times, seemingly taken by surprise, but rallied quickly. "We have many examples of investigations done on miracles."

"Miracles!" This outburst came from Lin, who rolled his eyes and slumped back as Arden raised his hand to quiet the junior professor.

Nalin continued undeterred. "The individuals tasked with these investigations were often the greatest skeptics." She cast a glance at Lin. "We can follow their example, even as we endeavor to keep our minds open to any possibility."

"Is the suggestion here that Geoff is a saint?" Lin asked, leaning forward and barely disguising the edge on his voice.

"Any possibility or no?" Nalin said, peevishly.

Lin scoffed and fell back into his chair again. Arden took it as a moment to step in. "I think we can all agree that any methods used in the past for trying to explain the inexplicable are of use to us here. Professor Nalin, can you construct a plan based on these methods?" A nod in response. "Professor Lin, can you focus on any way the boy may have encountered the story?"

Zeke spoke up quickly. "I should be the one..."

"Zeke," Arden interrupted. "I know, but it would be best to be as unbiased as possible in this regard."

"Am I not trusted?"

Arden rubbed his face. "Of course we trust you," he said.

"Do we?" The dry voice arriving unwanted.

"Professor bol Win!" Arden snapped at him before Zeke or Lin could react. "Really!" He brought his hand down on the table in front of him. "Professor Zeke," he said, firmly. "Please provide a compilation and analysis of Geoffrey's work over the past cycle."

"An entire cycle?" Lin spoke up on Zeke's behalf.

"We need to see if there has been a progression of his skill to arrive at this level naturally. Professor bol Win." He was speaking quickly to deter any additional interruption. "You will independently examine the work and conduct a similar analysis.

"Everyone else, please have an extended interview with your student. See if they have any knowledge at all. And prepare a detailed report for us to consider. Try to capture as much information as you can."

Arden paused and considered the faces pointed in his

direction. There were various levels of annoyance, frustration, interest, and even some anger, but they all showed confusion. None of them had the slightest idea. He sighed.

"Work as quickly as you can but thoroughly. Provide me with the results directly as soon as you're able. That will be all."

The Principal walked briskly on the pebbly path. Rust-colored rocks crunched under his feet, pressing into each other a bit more, being imperceptibly smoothed by the footfall. From above, looking straight down, the path around the school seemed to take unusual twists and turns. Giant boulders on the ground could scarcely be seen from such an angle, as their color and texture simply bled into the rest of the landscape. Red rocks and red dust and even often a red sky. Without context, a rock seen on the ground might be a few meters away and the size of a chair, or it might be a few hundred meters away, and the size of a dinner table. Depth perception was hopelessly muddled. The Principal liked to imagine he was on Mars.

His soft-soled sandals continued on, passing swiftly around the massive chunks of rock that dotted the harsh landscape, staying resolutely on the path that encircled it, looping the school as he had done thousands of times.

He knew each time he passed the spot where once there had been an intersection. Once, the path had split, and a branch had drifted off, up the ridge, eventually finding its way to the old road. It had been their physical link with all the rest of the whole world, but it was long since gone. Worn away by shifting dust, evaporating into memory.

Sometimes he could walk the loop for hours, and never spare a thought to the old path and the old road, to what lay outside his limited view. And sometimes he would walk by and be visited by memories and fantasies. Memories of when he traveled along such paths and the strange worlds and people he encountered; and fantasies of turning off, of finding the ghost of the trail leading to new adventures. But each time, the memories faded a bit more on the edges, and the fantasies seemed a bit more out of reach.

Still, the Principal walked, around and around his world, slowly grinding the rocks under his sandals into more dust.

How had he done it? And why? He must have known it would get discovered immediately. Le Fanu's collection of short stories certainly wasn't the most popular book in the library, but it was impossible to expect to be able to pass off as an original work. And what to do with the child? Teachers could be thrown out, but a student? A child? There was no precedent for it. Not for a case like this. How the devil had he done it?

As the Principal circled back to the front of the school, he saw Arden waiting on the path. When they got level, Arden nodded and stepped into pace with the Principal. The two walked in silence for a moment.

"Any insight then?" the Principal asked.

Before Arden could speak, he was interrupted by the Principal.

"Ach! Why do I even ask that? If there had been anything, you would have said something. But I have to ask like I'm reading a script. So we can have this needless exchange, wasting time on the expected mundanities while tiptoeing around the truth that we already know, which is that we have stumbled onto something we do not understand."

The two continued in silence again. Arden was a bit surprised at the outburst, but felt strangely relieved not to have to go through the motions of a rote conversation.

"How often do we say something pointless?" asked Arden.

"I go whole days without saying a single interesting word," the Principal grumbled. "Just repeating patterns of past conversations."

"I am afraid," - a muscle twitched in Arden's face - "that that is all my writing has become."

"I think that is all our fear."

After a few moments, Arden spoke. "How would you describe this? Their sandals crunched on the path?"

The Principal laughed. "That is exactly what I think to myself as I walk out here. My sandals crunching on the path."

"Such a good word though."

"Mm."

After another moment of walking, they both laughed.

"Can't get that word out of my head now," Arden said.

"What else? Tell me the scene."

"Let's see," Arden looked around. "A dusty wind blowing softly around the granite boulders. Pale sky."

"Pale sky. What's it like? What's it look like?"

"It's..." Arden looked up. "Soft. Like a, ah, a pale eggshell."

"Pale!"

"A tired eggshell? Wisps of cloud?"

"Wisps!" the Principal laughed.

"I can't help it!" Arden laughed along with him. "Clouds like, I don't know, pulled cotton."

The Principal sighed. "There's so much repetition, isn't there? So much of the familiar and the comfortable. How does the quote go?" He stared up at the sky. "All things are wearisome, more than one can describe; the eye is not satisfied with seeing, nor the ear content with hearing. What has been will be again, and what has been done will be done again; there is nothing new under the sun." He scoffed. "How many times have we seen clouds described as wisps? But how many times have we looked up at the clouds, and that's just what they look like? That's what the bloody things are, day after day. How can we write something new when we can't even live something new?"

"Mm," Arden murmured in agreement. "And here we're trying to have these kids do the same? What have they lived? And now this," he trailed off.

The two men continued in silence beneath the wisps of clouds.

"When I was little," Arden said. "I would be working on maths and I'd come to a problem I couldn't solve. Well, I'd come to lots of problems I couldn't solve." The Principal chuckled. "But sometimes, I'd come to one that I knew absolutely didn't make any sense. That even when I knew the answer, it didn't follow from the rules of mathematics. And I'd get so excited, because I thought I'd stumbled across some fundamental mistake in the universe. Something that didn't fit with anything known. Something new. Would you believe I was always wrong?"

The Principal chuckled again. "Every time?"

"Every time."

"So is that the lesson? We think we've stumbled onto something profound, but there's really some explanation?"

"Oh, there's some explanation regardless."

"Some reasonable explanation then. Something that fits with our known universe."

"I'd get older, and those moments got fewer and fewer. But I always felt that excitement. Until I got a little older still. Then I'd start to feel scared, and I would feel relief when I inevitably learned that the rules of the world hadn't been broken, instead of disappointment."

The Principal looked over at Arden. The man's eyes were looking far away, or far backwards, or far inwards. "And are you scared now?" The Principal saw crinkles appear under Arden's eyes.

"No," he said, and the rest of the smile came to his face. "I feel excited. Thrilled. Isn't that silly?"

The Principal made a small, surprised sound. "Why silly?"

"Well, we didn't really find a hole in the universe, did we? There will be some mundane explanation. Something that makes sense. Every magic trick has a solution that ruins the trick."

"It's certainly a clever trick," the Principal murmured. "It does feel different though, doesn't it. Feels special. Or maybe it's just the moment before the magic curtain is lifted."

"Mm."

"A hole in the universe?"

"Oh," Arden laughed. "That's just what I imagined it was when I was a child. That I would look in some hidden corner that no one had ever looked in before, and I would find it. Evidence that what we thought we knew was all wrong. A hole in the universe."

"You were quite the child," the Principal said, and they both laughed.

Geoffrey stared at the task list. Laundry.

It was usually a coveted chore. It was indoors, first of all. The room was warm and humid, and there was water close by. Most of all though, it was mindless. You could let your mind wander, conjuring up ideas and phrases, characters and stories. It was where countless books had started. But letting his mind wander was the last thing that Geoffrey wanted. He wanted a distraction. Something to focus on that wasn't his conversation with the Principal. He stared at the list. Gardening. Pency. That was good, wasn't it?

Geoffrey sighed and turned around. The barracks were empty. Everyone was probably out in the yard. He just had to go out and ask Pency to trade. Pency'd jump at the chance. Gardening for laundry? There wasn't a better trade than that. All he had to do was ask.

Geoffrey didn't move.

Instead, his gaze started to slowly track across the room.

Seeing the rows of beds, the dark blue covers, all tightly tucked and smoothed. The white walls where they would make finger shadow animals when the sun came through the window just right. The dark ceiling that made the whole room seem lower than it really was. His eye stopped at his bed, third from the door, on the left side. His bed for now. His books in his cabinet, along with three extra habits. Under his pillow, a dream journal. His writing journal in its side pocket, hanging off the mattress. An extra journal underneath the mattress and three more blanks in the back of his cabinet. His soap and brushes and papers in his medical box under the bed.

Were they going to kick him out? Would he have to pack up all his things? Where would he put them? How could he carry them? Where would he go? This was his home. That was his bed. There wasn't anything else.

They had said he wasn't being expelled. They said it and they couldn't take it back. Could they? What if they changed their minds? That's what they're meeting about, probably.

The tightness came back to his chest, making it difficult to breathe. What if this was the last time he looked at his room? The last time he had his things?

Finally, the agony of standing in the empty room grew greater than his fear of going out to the yard and he hurried out of the barracks. In the corridor, the pain dissipated somewhat but Geoffrey couldn't shake the thought that every view of the school would be the last time he'd ever have that particular view. Each stone he stepped on was the last time he would step on it. He knew he shouldn't run but there was no rule about walking fast. Geoffrey sped toward the yard.

The students were huddled around the stones' diagrams. It looked like two games were going on. Pency had his back to Geoffrey.

Geoffrey stepped slowly onto the cobblestones, cold even through his sandals. This time of year, it was calm. Light came through the great windows and could even be a little warm if you stayed in the bright long enough. In a season, the winds would start up again and all they could do was fly paper kites before they were torn to bits by the dust, or play scarecrow if the teachers weren't around. They'd had to stop that when Stephen was temporarily blinded. His eyesight had come back though. The fuss seemed overblown.

Geoffrey was stalling. Several students had noticed him already. Wint's head had jerked slightly and a few more had noticed and looked discreetly over at him. Pency's stance almost imperceptibly shifted, even with his back to Geoffrey. It was like a klaxon had gone off that they were all trying to ignore. Geoffrey sighed and walked toward the group.

Mart was playing Shinty and Lulu was playing Stephen. The others had circled around the four players squatting on the ground, their two boards side-by-side. Geoffrey stood next to Pency. No one said anything. The stones clicked on the ground. Shinty missed a shot and hissed, glaring at Geoffrey for the distraction.

It was very awkward.

"Pency," Geoffrey said. Pency didn't react. "Trade you for laundry."

Several students looked over, wondering how Pency would respond. It felt like a test. Pency stared passively down at the games as Mart moved. The wait extended and Geoffrey felt worse and worse. He felt like he was standing outside a house he used to live in, staring in through a window at his old family. Finally Pency shrugged.

"Fine."

Stephen groaned. "Honestly?"

"Play your game," Pency said, flatly.

"Thanks, Pency," Geoffrey said.

"Thanks, Pency," Stephen mimicked.

Pency's face didn't change. "I'm not turning down laundry for gardening, you idiot."

"So you deal with a cheat?"

"I'm not a cheat!" Geoffrey shouted.

Lulu shifted, annoyed. "Would you go already?" she muttered to Stephen. Many of the students were looking at the space between their feet. Mart was staring intently at her board while Shinty sighed audibly. A chill breeze had picked up and pushed steadily through the yard. Geoffrey's eyes darted across the scene. Stephen seemed to be the only one hot. Shinty was a little annoyed but not overly, and everyone else just looked concerned. Maybe everyone didn't hate him. He looked evenly back at Stephen and took a deep breath.

"I didn't cheat," Geoffrey said.

Now Greta looked over. "You know I read it once? Carmilla? Ages ago. They questioned me for hours about it. I hardly even remember it. But they kept asking me if I copied it for you. Or told you about it."

Geoffrey stood there, blinking.

"I can't go to the library now," Greta said.

"None of us can," added Shinty.

Geoffrey's mouth was dry. "I'm sorry," he said, softly.

"Just," Mart spoke loudly, then quieted, catching herself. "Just tell them. It will be okay. We'll understand. Tell them how you did it."

"And an uncanny job of it," Wint muttered. There were murmurs of agreement. Pency turned to him.

"How did you do it?" he asked, emphasizing the second word.

"I don't fucking believe this," Stephen cursed.

"Just shut up," Mart said. "He made a mistake."

Geoffrey stood, petrified. "But," he said. They weren't mad. They were his friends. They were standing by him. But they all thought he had cheated. Had plagiarized. It was the worst thing any of them could do, to steal the art of another and pass it off as their own. To shame their school and disrespect their own words and their own minds. It was all so important, all the work they were doing. They were writing, telling stories. Stories to inspire and entertain. Stories to teach and open minds, stories to lift people across the stars. Stories to carry on humanity when humanity had seemed all but lost. And to cheapen it with plagiarism was an unholy crime. Even then though, his schoolmates were standing by him. Most of them anyway. It meant a great deal to Geoffrey and he struggled with the next words. "I didn't cheat."

Stephen laughed.

"Come on, Geoff," Mart said.

The yard was quiet. The breeze had finally passed on, winding its way through the rocks surrounding the school. There was compassion in Mart's eyes as she looked at Geoffrey. The rest of the students stared at him with mixtures of care, pity, and disappointment. Stephen alone had contempt. None of them believed him.

Geoffrey took a step back. Mart's brow creased together; her eyes confused now, quizzical. He felt hot now, burning up, and crushed like he was in a vice.

"Thanks, Pence," he gasped, and fled.

"I have requested help," the Principal said.

The Assembly Room was half empty, populated as it was with only teachers. The Principal stood at the narrow grey lectern, looking out at the semicircle of rows of tables. He had paused, intentionally, wondering what kind of reaction that might solicit, but also for a bit of dramatic effect, if he was being perfectly honest. His audience remained impassive. The Principal continued, slightly dejected.

"Our Superintendent has agreed and is sending an

investigator. They will arrive in time. Until then, we will continue with writing exercises. Perhaps some good content will come from all this."

He paused again, looking at the faces of the teachers; his teachers. Those faces hung low, weary, depressed.

"An investigator?" It was Arden. "Is that really necessary?"

"Yes," said the Principal, in acknowledgment, if not agreement. "Well, perhaps not. I thought it a bit much. I hadn't expected," he trailed off, distracted again, before bringing himself back. "Something so formal. But there was a team close by. An investigator and three officers."

"Officers?" Arden protested again. The Principal nodded. "Central Authority is sending officers here?" There were murmurs among the other teachers.

"Doesn't that strike you as a bit hasty?" bol Win asked.

Nalin was next. "What will it mean to the school now that a case of plagiarism has been reported?"

"We could be dismantled," Lin said.

This led to another chaotic outburst from the assembled faculty. The Principal turned his face down, staring at the bare lectern. Speckled wear marks traced a vague outline of a page. How many times had he stood here, rested his hands on the plastic, shuffled his notes? He ran his thumb down the side, feeling the tiny imperfections along the edge. How long had they tried to solve this puzzle on their own before he had asked for help from the board? How long ago had he asked? How long had he been standing there? The cacophony grew louder.

"Please," said the Principal, holding his hands up. He blinked, taking in the scene in front of him. A room of people, upset, all talking at once, not hearing, not listening, only a jumbled mess that each one would recognize as counterproductive if they were being objective. And there he was, at the head of the room, bestowed the role of the person who raised their hands to instill order in the unruly group. How many times? How many times had it happened? How many times had he read such a scene?

They would respond to the gesture because they all knew the scene too. It was a comfort, a scheme in their minds to play along with, to take away the stress of having to decide a course of action of one's own. Their responses were preselected for them, and there was a relief to that. It meant a comfort for him as well. Not only were his choices prescribed, but he knew that the proper sequence would allow him to successfully corral everyone in the room. All he had to do was follow the correct steps.

The Principal slowly realized that the room had quieted again. He looked out onto the puzzled and concerned faces all directed at him. As though from a distance, he saw his arms were still outstretched. He was standing like a scarecrow. The gesture had been the right one but he had held it for too long without pairing it with the correct speech models. Now he felt like he was dangling on frozen marionette strings, unable to detach himself.

"Principal?"

Zeke's kind voice cut through the paralysis, freeing his body and allowing his arms to return to his sides. In the silence, he turned and slipped out of the room.

Zeke and Lin found him wandering the halls. He started back and forth, his hands constantly working, wringing one hand then the next. The hallway was cold and it was evening. The Principal looked this way and that, deep creases on his forehead. As the pair of teachers approached, he looked up, noticing them. In his eyes, briefly, was a mixture of confusion and hope. A desperate naivete, it seemed to Zeke.

"Oh," the Principal said.

He stopped his agitated pacing and cast about, as though

he was looking for a chair. Stepping back, as if it was the most natural thing in the world, he leaned against the wall and slid down to the cold tile stone floor, his habit bunching around him. Zeke and Lin looked quickly at each other, then away.

Zeke squatted down in front of the Principal. She could see his eyes, still wandering, but they suddenly set on her.

The two stared at each other in silence. Side by side, but a world apart.

Zeke saw the outline of the man before her. She looked for signs that he may be unwell. She looked with care and concern. She saw the strange cast in his eyes, the rapid rise and fall of his chest, a dot of sweat, despite the chill, on this temple. She noted no discoloration of his eyes or on his skin, no odor of malaise on his breath. His habit and hands were clean; he was not neglecting his hygiene. He was clearly under a great deal of stress, but there was no major cause for alarm. That was what she saw.

The Principal saw light blonde hair contrasting so strongly against dark skin. Among the yellow strands, he saw pure white, almost perfectly hidden. There were the epicanthic folds over eyes that were mostly brown. But close around the pupil of the right eye was an uneven patch of green. No, it would have been her left eye, wouldn't it? A few red veins throughout the white of her eye, and all surrounded by short lashes. Such a complex combination of traits; her family must have had a talented geneticist. Unless her hair had started to turn white prematurely, which was unlikely, she had probably waited a little extra longer than most before getting her dose. That was what he saw.

Lin saw Zeke and the Principal looking at each other.

"Zeke," said the Principal.

"Yes?" she asked. The care and concern in her eyes was matched with her voice.

"Zeke," he repeated, softly, as though it were occurring to

him for the first time.

"Principal," Zeke said, worry creeping into her voice.

"Where on earth did you get your name?"

Zeke and Lin both blinked.

"My name?"

The Principal nodded slowly and closed his eyes. "Yes, please."

"It's," Zeke paused, confused. "It was my grandfather's."

The Principal nodded, his eyes still closed. Then his forehead creased. "But why name their daughter that?"

"Well," she paused again. "They thought I would be a boy."

The Principal's eyes opened, but his face crinkled more. Lin looked at Zeke with slight surprise.

"Why did they think that?" the Principal asked.

Zeke sat back on her heels and stared at the Principal. He had asked the question with such a strange sincerity. Like it mattered more to him than anything else in the world. She shrugged. "The test was wrong."

"Wrong?" the Principal exclaimed. "Wasn't your geneticist controlling it?"

Zeke smiled. "No. My parents left gender up to chance."

"Oh," the Principal said. "Do you know why?"

"My mother said they controlled so much, they wanted something left to be decided by the universe."

Now the Principal smiled. "I like that," he said. "But the test?"

"Yes, the prenatal scan was just wrong. They thought I was a boy and settled on the name. When I showed up, they got a bit of a shock, but they wanted to keep the name."

"The test was just wrong?" the Principal asked, amused.

Zeke shrugged again. "Hospital said it can happen sometimes."

The Principal laughed. "It can happen? The odds must be

astronomical."

"My father used to say I was one in a million," Zeke said softly, smiling.

The Principal heard the pain in her voice and took her hand. "And indeed you are," he said. "This one thinks so too," he jerked his head at Lin.

Zeke laughed brightly as Lin looked away. "Don't you worry," Zeke said. "I'm not about to violate protocol."

"Oh," the Principal sighed. "Isn't that a pity."

"Come on now," Zeke stood and gently helped the Principal up. The three started to slowly walk back to quarters.

"Bit of an age difference, isn't there?" the Principal asked. "How old were you?" he asked Zeke.

"Forty-three," she said. He had been right; she had waited.

"And you?" he asked, looking at Lin. He seemed quite young, and square-headed. Solid, the Principal might have said. If he was honest, the Principal wouldn't have believed the man was a teacher.

"Twenty-three," Lin said, quietly. Zeke looked straight ahead, passive. She had known that already. The Principal turned to Lin.

"October seven." he said. Of course. He had forgotten.

"Mm," Lin said.

"Oh, my boy," the Principal said, and took his hand as they walked.

The three continued down the hall.

The Principal glanced to Zeke. "Have I ever asked you about your name before?"

"Not that I can recall."

TWO
THE INVESTIGATOR

Geoffrey was half-walking half-running again. He hurried down halls trying not to break into a flat out sprint. Passing quickly through a door he went up an enclosed circular staircase. There were no lights, only small slits on one side of the curved wall letting in some unfiltered light. It was dim and the steps were awkward causing Geoffrey to scuff his shin more than once in his rush.

Reaching the top, he burst through the door onto the roof and into bright light. He ran now to the edge of the building, small pebbles lodging between his toes. There was a low wall that ringed the gravel-covered roof. On the other side of the school, there was a garden, but nothing was growing there now. Geoffrey threw himself against the wall, draping his arms over the stone. He stared out over the red landscape to the ridge.

It was kilometers away but felt to Geoffrey like it was looming over him. He stared at the flat line at the top. It was broken by a few boulders that must have been massive but there was nothing else. No scrub brush. No movement. Geoffrey knew that all the world lay beyond that ridge. Past that line, somewhere, were trees and cities, people, cars and trains, houses, rocket ships, tigers, spices, holographics, circuses, robots, and everything else in the whole world that didn't exist at his small school.

Geoffrey had never seen the ridge line broken. Once, their supply airdrop had malfunctioned and a ground transport had been sent. Everyone had been excited to see the vehicle but all Geoffrey had wanted was to see it crest that ridge. Just to see evidence that the outside world really existed. On the scheduled day, he had been folding clothes when the transport arrived. It was early. Their shipment was unloaded and the transport departed before he had even heard about it.

Was any of it real? Was there really something out there or was it all just in their books now? Just stories.

No one knew exactly when the investigator would arrive but they would have to come over that ridge. And Geoffrey desperately wanted to see it.

The door opened behind him and he heard footfalls on the gravel. He glanced back and saw Pency walking toward him. Geoffrey returned to his view. Pency flopped across the wall next to him.

"Any sign of them yet?" Pency asked.

"Uh uh."

They stood there, leaning on the cool stone, peering almost absent-mindedly over the harsh landscape, which to them was simply normal. Their habits were identical and they shared the same closely cropped hair, as every student did. Similar backgrounds lent both boys a soft caramel skin tone; a candy that neither of them had ever seen, let alone tasted. Both had brown eyes. An observer would have difficulty in telling them apart. Pency was slightly taller; Geoffrey seemed a bit rounder, but that was only due to the shape of his face.

They kicked at the gravel under their identical sandals.

"What are you going to tell them?" Pency asked.

"Tell who?"

Both Geoffrey and Pency were speaking flatly.

"The investigator."

Geoffrey shrugged. "Same thing I told everybody else. Why wouldn't I?" A defensive edge slipped into his voice.

Pency sighed. "Come on, Geoff." Now an exasperated tone was added to Pency's.

"What?"

"You know what."

"No, I don't. Why don't you tell me."

Pency grunted and pushed himself away from the wall. He walked a few steps away. "Stop being such a shitbrain," he said. "I'm tired of defending you all the time. Just tell the truth."

Geoffrey stayed wrapped over the wall. "I am telling the truth," he said, clenching his teeth. "And I never asked you to defend me."

Pency turned and stared at his back. Geoffrey remained looking out at the ridge. Pency closed the distance between them quickly and pushed Geoffrey hard.

"Hey!" Geoffrey shouted, his feet sliding on the small stones underfoot.

Pency pushed him again, and Geoffrey fell to the ground. In a moment he was back up, throwing himself at Pency. The two shoved each other with no real malice. They quieted.

"You didn't copy it?" Pency asked, in a way that suggested very strongly that Geoffrey had indeed copied it. "You just happened to make up, word for word, the exact same story as one written who knows how many cycles ago?"

"Yes!" Geoffrey shouted. "I know it's crazy. But I'd never read it. I just thought it up."

The two boys stared at each other. Pency cursed and looked up at the sky.

"Please," said Geoffrey. "I'm telling the truth."

Bright sun shot through the clouds. A wind crept gently up and washed over the roof. Their habits fluttered in sync with one another. The gravel had once been white but was now ingrained with the same red dust they kicked up with every step, causing the bottoms of all the habits to be perpetually tinged, like sunset.

Pency suddenly shouted, breaking the calm. "Stop lying!"

"I'm not lying!" Geoffrey shouted back. Their voices were loud in their heads but died quickly on the wind.

"Everybody knows it," Pency said, still angry. "Do you know how much I've had to defend you? Do you have any idea how much I've stood up for you?" Geoffrey's eyes were wide and pain was on his face. "I don't care!" Pency shouted. "I don't care. It's just a dumb mistake. It's okay, okay? Stop making it worse. The Principal said you could still stay. But what about the investigator?" Geoffrey still just stared. "If you don't talk to them, if you don't tell the truth, they could expel you. They'll figure out how you did it and they'll ship you off somewhere. Come on, Geoff!"

The thought tugged at the inside of Geoffrey's chest. He could just say he copied it. They'd stop asking questions. And it would all fade away eventually. Wouldn't it? Or would it follow him endlessly? Now Pency was staring at him with desperation in his eyes. Geoffrey looked down.

"I didn't," he said, softly.

Pency exploded. "Stop being such a fucking liar!"

Geoffrey's fist struck Pency high on his left cheek. Pency's eyes went wide and then he swung back, his forearm glancing over Geoffrey's head. In a moment the two were on the ground, elbows and knees hitting relentlessly. The gravel was painful and bit at their skin through the cloth habits. Pency had a cut over his eye and blood welled up. Geoffrey hesitated at the sight of it letting Pency have a brief window. A compact punch into Geoffrey's stomach left him struggling to breathe.

Pency pushed himself free and stood. He looked down at his friend, bent double on his side, mouth wide, emitting short gasps that sent puffs of red clouds into the air. Pency gritted his teeth.

"Breathe through your mouth," he said, and walked off.

During the fight, Geoffrey had missed the sight of a small

group come into view over the ridge line and begin to descend.

The Investigator sat in the Principal's office scanning through images on a thin tablet. Her team of three officers stood behind, despite the two empty chairs next to the Investigator. One looked absent-mindedly at the titles of the books on the shelves. Arden sat in the chair in the corner. The Principal sat behind the desk.

"And the boy?" the Investigator asked without looking up.

"Well," said the Principal. "Geoffrey's been with us since just after he received treatment."

The Investigator glanced up. "That long?" she asked. "Is that normal?"

"Yes," said the Principal. "It's the same for all the students."

The Investigator murmured and returned to the tablet.

"Yes," the Principal said again, after a short pause when he thought the Investigator was waiting for him to continue. "He's shown an aptitude for free writing, so he hasn't read quite as much as some of the other students. Still quite well-read, of course. I think he averages one to two disciplinary actions every cycle or so, which is on the low side."

"Anything significant?" the Investigator asked.

"Oh, no," said the Principal. "Minor rule infraction. The occasional schoolyard scrap. That kind of thing. You know."

The Investigator looked up, now with a bemused expression. "I can't say that I do," she said. "Anything related to writing?"

"No, no," the Principal shook his head. "Nothing remotely like this."

The Investigator nodded. "And how is his writing?"

"Quite strong," said the Principal. "He does best with iambic pentameter and a play format but his short stories are also well done. Um," the Principal paused. The Investigator waited. "Nothing, I would say, at the level of Carmilla," said the Principal. "Even if none of us had read it the piece would have stood out. He's still an unpolished talent."

The Investigator nodded again and a flicker crossed her brow for a moment before she turned back to her tablet. The stylus glided noiselessly over the screen and there was silence in the room. Eventually she stopped and looked up. She faced the Principal but her eyes were directed slightly down and to his right. The Principal glanced furtively to try to see what she was looking at.

There was a pause before she spoke. "We haven't dealt much with children," she said finally.

"But you've had plagiarism cases before, yes?" asked Arden from the corner.

"It doesn't come up with great frequency," the Investigator said, slightly sardonically, the Principal thought. "And there doesn't seem much in this case that is in question. Here, you know the work, you know where the only copy is, and there's been no real attempt to hide the crime." The Investigator paused. "Is this... child-like?"

"I'm sorry, I don't," the Principal trailed off.

"Have you dealt with children?" Arden paused for emphasis. "At all?"

Now the Investigator turned fully, looking directly back at Arden. The Principal saw her jawbone tighten. After a beat, Arden looked down. The Investigator turned back to the Principal. "I have questions about development."

"Whatever I can do," the Principal replied hurriedly.

The Investigator tapped her stylus on the screen. Now the mood in the room was uncomfortable. "What is the mental development of the students here? And of Geoffrey?" the Investigator asked, her questions flat and to the point.

"Our students all have a developmental age of twelve years, roughly," said the Principal.

The Investigator looked aggravated. "Developmental age," she said. "That is physical, yes?"

"Physical," agreed the Principal. "And mental. Emotional. That is how old they are."

"Mentally," said the Investigator.

"Yes," said the Principal. He was growing more and more uncomfortable.

"But," the Investigator paused. "How old are they?" she asked, pointedly.

Arden made a startled sound. "Weren't you briefed on this?"

The Investigator's eyes closed. The Principal flinched internally. He could feel frustration radiate off of her.

"We were diverted," said the officer who was still perusing the bookshelves. "Coming home after spending the last half cycle on assignment on the pole." He turned and looked at Arden. "On our way back to rest."

The Principal suddenly felt like he wasn't really there. Like he was just an observer. He watched the scene play out, like a comfort. The tempered annoyance, bravado, challenges. The officer - what was his name? It had been given on arrival, but it had melted away. It was something strange. That one felt the need to display his authority over the naive school teacher. He had a strange way of moving; it was very fluid, almost like a cat, if he was remembering cats properly. There was a strength and a confidence there. But Arden could certainly hold his own with biting jabs. The two might get along if they spent more time together. The dynamic was so typical. As the predictable conversation moved toward its inevitable conclusion, the Principal gazed around the room as if for the first time.

Here were four people in his office who had never been there before. This was the first time his office had ever existed in this configuration. He was so used to seeing the simple habits the teachers and students all wore that the drab grey uniforms of the Investigator and her officers looked quite out of place. The one jawing with Arden looked like a soldier but certainly wasn't. He was too gregarious. But he had that same cast, like Lin and Arden both. Not tall, not short, not bulky, not lanky. Solid. And the same pale brown skin, slightly mottled, as apparently this provided the best base for camouflage, of all the awful things. This one and Lin kept their hair cropped short, though Arden's was longer.

The Principal stared at the other two officers, trying to take in their appearance to atone for forgetting their names. The one closest to the Investigator – another former soldier but completely bald. Three straight thin tattooed lines ran the length of his head from front to back, ending just where his hairline would have been. He was staring at the argumentative one now with a look that seemed to be both amused and annoyed. That was quite a feat. The last officer simply looked bored, but at least he didn't resemble the others. It might have been difficult to tell them apart. What was this one's name? Something with a B. He had curly hair like the Principal hadn't seen since before he came to this school. It was a deep brown and matched his skin almost perfectly. Perhaps a shade or two darker.

Something caught his eye. Dust motes were swirling in the light. Dust motes. How often had he watched them? Countless times. And each time he called them dust motes in his head. Each time he made mention of them in a story, he called them dust motes, and wrote how they swirled in the light. Wasn't there something else to call them? Some other to describe them? Specks? Fluttering? It sounded wrong, didn't it? He wondered when he had first seen the word written down. His eye followed a mote as it skipped and jumped on invisible currents. It crossed in front of the face of the Investigator and vanished. The Investigator's eyes were still closed.

"This is where I provide exposition, isn't it?" the Principal asked, softly. "About the school."

Her eyes opened. Arden and the officer were still bickering. "I would appreciate it, yes," she said. The officer registered the sound of her voice and stopped talking, turned. The room was silent again.

"Because you don't know," said the Principal. "Because you were diverted." The corners of the Investigator's eyes turned up. "They didn't give you a case file?" the Principal asked. The Investigator remained silent, but her eyes still danced, just a little. "They did, didn't they?" the Principal said. "With our report?"

The Investigator nodded once, slowly.

"Can we just skip this?" the Principal asked.

The Investigator raised an eyebrow. "Skip?"

"This," the Principal waved his hand again. "All this talk."

"I would like to hear your version," the Investigator said, almost apologetically.

The Principal sighed. "What do you know already?" What had been in that blasted report?

The Investigator smiled slightly. "I prefer not to cross contaminate my information streams," she said.

"Ah," said the Principal. "Of course." He rubbed his face. "I'll be self-conscious about it now," he said, almost to himself. He looked at Arden. "Bring bol Win, would you?" he asked.

Arden stood, looking confused, and departed.

The Principal looked at the officers. "I've forgotten all of your names," he said.

Professor Zeke stared at her ward. He was sitting at his desk, reading. His writing journal lay next to him, unopened. Whenever he read something, no matter what it was, three lines appeared across his forehead in concentration. They would get more pronounced if something scary was happening, and less if something funny was happening.

When she had arrived at this school, they had given her a file on her mentee. It had information about his writing skill and reading level and what books he seemed to prefer and what writers he seemed to take after. But it hadn't included anything about the boy himself. Not really. She had had to learn on her own what his favorite book really was, and what author he admired the most. She had learned that he chewed his pencil when he was angry at what he had written, and would set it down next to him when he was sad at what he had written. She had learned that he didn't remember anything before coming to this school. Perhaps that was for the best though.

All the students here so closely resembled each other, she had to find some deviations to tell them apart. How they carried themselves, how they sounded. She thought it would be impossible when she first arrived, but it turned out to be remarkably easy. Each student was so different from the other in so many ways outside of their similar appearances. And besides, even then there were small deviations. A tiny sliver of a bald spot was on the back of Geoffrey's head; she had thought it a scar somehow when she first saw him, but of course that was impossible.

He turned a page, and sighed, and looked away. Probably a chapter break. "How is it?" she asked.

Geoffrey shrugged. "It's good, I guess." He looked back at the book. "It's a little strange. When does Prometheus show up?"

Professor Zeke smiled to herself. "Well, he doesn't. It's just an expression here."

"Oh," Geoffrey said, looking disappointed. He stared back at the book. "They can't really do that, can they?"

"Do what?"

"Take different dead people and stitch them together and make a new one?"

"No," said Professor Zeke. "It's just a story."

"Oh," he said, again. "I didn't think so." He was quiet. "Can you imagine what they'd look like? All scars covering them." He bit his lip.

"Have you written anything recently?"

His face changed. His whole body changed. He drew inward on himself and stared down at his lap. "No," he said, softly.

"Geoffrey," she started.

"I'd just like to focus on reading for a while now if that's okay," he said quickly.

She crumpled a little bit inside. He seemed so much in pain. "That's fine," she said. But she didn't want to make it seem like she was giving him special treatment. He wouldn't like that. "For a while. We'll get back to some writing exercises in a bit, okay?"

He looked up and gave a small smile. "Thank you," he said. "Could," he started and stopped. She opened her eyes a little wider and waited. "Could I write, when I write, just about me?"

"About you? Of course," she said. "You mean living here?"

"Well," he shifted in his seat, looking uncomfortable. "Yeah. And about the kids here. And what, what happened to us."

This was different. Professor Zeke leaned back. Geoffrey stared at the floor. "What happened to you?" she prompted.

"Yeah, with how we got here and everything," he said, carefully, still staring at the floor.

She hesitated. "Do you... know how you got here?"

He looked miserable. "No," he dragged out the word. "Not really. Could I," he swallowed. "Could I learn about that? Read about it?"

How was she supposed to tell him that his own past was a secret that even she didn't have access to? Not that she hadn't been able to guess. For all the children here. But there was no book he could read for that. She sighed.

"Nevermind," he said quickly, opening his book back up. No sense in getting himself into even more trouble.

Arden knocked once and entered, followed by Professor bol Win. The older teacher looked flustered. The Principal rose and walked around his desk to the middle of the room. The Investigator remained seated, but turned halfway to partially face the rest of the room.

"Professor bol Win," said the Principal, both as greeting and introduction.

The three officers nodded and the bald one stepped forward, raising his hand, palm inward to chest in a formal greeting that neither bol Win, Arden, nor the Principal were familiar with. "Officer Tyrick," he said.

"Officer Brighton," said the second officer, the one with curly hair, with the same salute.

"Officer Third," said the last officer, the one who had been staring at the books and had the spat with Arden.

"Officer?" bol Win looked even more flustered. "Third?"

"Yes," said Third. "It means tertius."

There was a pause. The Principal smiled slightly and shook his head at the bizarre joke, delivered in deadpan. Bol Win stood stunned.

"Yes," said the Principal. "And this is the lead investigator for our case." He motioned to the Investigator who stood, and nodded once to bol Win.

"Investigator?" bol Win trailed off, expectantly.

"Yes," said the Investigator, ignoring the question. "I wanted to get some more information on this school and the students. Your Principal recommended you."

Bol Win nodded graciously to the Principal. "Anything I can do," he said.

"Shall we take this outside?" said the Principal. "We're a bit crowded here, and a walk around the grounds could provide a helpful setting."

The Investigator nodded, and turned to the officers. "You don't have to stick around. Feel free to peruse on your own. With your permission, of course," she said, looking at the Principal.

He smiled slightly. As though he could refuse. "Of course," he said.

THREE

THE GREENHOUSE

Geoffrey crouched over the vegetable garden bed, pulling weeds. White light bathed him, filtering in through the great greenhouse windows. He was in the carrot section, plucking dandelion greens for supper. Behind him, the door slid open. Geoffrey glanced back and saw Lulu enter and walk toward the cucumbers with a hose. He turned back to the dandelions while she began watering her section.

Mart had been on the board. Maybe she and Lulu had traded. That would be a little strange. Mart already owed Lulu. Maybe Lulu was being generous. Geoffrey continued down the line.

The door opened again and Mart came in. She walked to the cucumbers, carrying a trowel. Geoffrey stood, stretching his back. "Hey," he said, uncertainly. Neither Mart or Lulu looked at him, or even each other. They were simply gardening.

The door opened again and Shinty came in, carrying shears. He walked to the perennials and began pruning.

Before Geoffrey could move, the door was opening again and Stephen walked in, carrying nothing. He strode directly past Geoffrey to the end of the carrot line, and began pulling dandelion leaves. Geoffrey looked down, dumbly, at the leaves still in his hand. The sound of the door opening again made him wince. This time, Greta, Wint, and Max came in, followed by Pency.

Every student was in the greenhouse. During chores. Now they were all looking at him. They had snuck out here? All of them? For what?

Stephen walked slowly down the carrot line toward him. Geoffrey's eyes darted around the greenhouse, and fell on Pency. Pency just stared at him. Geoffrey felt his chest tighten. Stephen approached and stopped a few feet from him.

Geoffrey became very aware of the smell of the dirt and dandelion leaves in his hand.

"You're a plagiarist," said Stephen.

"I'm not!" Geoffrey said, instinctively.

"Shut up," Stephen said. It sounded like an order. Geoffrey looked at all the faces staring at him. They all looked the same. They all looked cold. A gust of wind momentarily shook the greenhouse windows, clattering.

Geoffrey ran. Wint moved quickly and grabbed Geoffrey's left arm, and he ran into Pency, who shoved him back. Max grabbed his right arm. And there was Stephen's face, sneering and shouting. "Shinty!" And there was Shinty, still holding the shears. Geoffrey felt panic. He dug his feet into the ground and tried to push backward, but Wint and Max were too strong. They held him tight, their hands under his shoulders, fingers digging painfully into his armpits. The other students were just staring. Pency was just staring. No one was helping him. He was alone.

"Stop it," Stephen said, softly but cruelly. Geoffrey stopped struggling. "Let him go," said Stephen. Max and Wint let his arms drop. Geoffrey stood there, in the bright greenhouse, trampled greens under his feet, surrounded by his friends. He couldn't stop his breath or his heart from speeding up, tightening. "Hold out your hand," said Stephen.

"What?"

"Hold out," Stephen repeated. "Your hand."

In Geoffrey's mind and written on his face was nothing but confusion, panic, and fear. He reacted in a confused, panicked, and fearful manner, even as he complied thoughtlessly. If he had been thinking clearly, he might not have reacted the same way. Perhaps if he was older, he would have retained some autonomy. But he is only a child, after all. They are all only children.

Geoffrey's hand slowly came up. His arm was bent slightly at the elbow, and his palm was facing up, the hand slightly cupped. Stephen looked away to Shinty, then back to Geoffrey.

"Cut off a finger," said Stephen.

"What?" Geoffrey asked, loudly. He jerked his hand back to his side, but made no other movement. No step back. No one else moved.

"Hold out!" Stephen repeated. "Your hand!"

"No!" Geoffrey finally protested.

Stephen took two steps forward very quickly. Geoffrey blinked, leaning back slightly. "You do it," hissed Stephen. "You do it or we will never talk to you ever again."

"What?" Geoffrey gasped. He didn't even mean to. It was all he could do. He wanted to look around to see the faces of everyone who must have agreed to this ultimatum. He wanted to look at Pency. But all he could was stare into Stephen's eyes. They were a dark brown usually, but in the bright light of the greenhouse, they were much softer. Geoffrey could see ridges and whorls in the cornea. He was looking for some hope, some deeper meaning than what was being presented to him. But he found nothing. To him, it may as well have been a glass eye.

Stephen took two steps backward, evenly.

"Hold out your hand," said Stephen.

The room was still again. Geoffrey looked to Shinty, and to the pruning shears in his hand. Geoffrey had cut through branches thicker than his thumbs with them. He wondered how strong bone was compared to a living branch. He thought about the last time he had sharpened the blades, turning them to a razor's edge. Geoffrey thought about which hand he wanted to keep whole.

Very slowly, he raised his left hand. His arm was straight, palm facing down. He hoped Shinty would cut the pinkie. Stephen nodded to Shinty, who brought the shears up and held them over Geoffrey's pinkie. Geoffrey felt a sense of relief, just for a moment.

"You stole the words of another," Stephen intoned. "You took a story that wasn't yours and passed it off as your own. You threatened the integrity of the work that we all do. You bring pride and greed to the work of truth-telling." Geoffrey remembered, as they all did, the lesson on plagiarism. Stephen's paraphrase continued. "You tried to reshape the past, to take the wisdom of another and pretend it was your own." Geoffrey thought to himself that the correct word from their lesson had been 'turn', not 'take'. "Without that integrity, you threaten the present and the future. Without that integrity, you threaten all of us." Geoffrey stared blankly at his fingers, feeling the edge of the shears.

He knew plagiarism was the worst thing anyone could do at the school. He knew the punishment was fair. He closed his eyes.

"Unless," Stephen said suddenly. Geoffrey opened his eyes. "You confess and tell us how you did it."

Geoffrey's chin dropped to his chest and two tears fell to the ground. "I didn't do it," he whispered.

"Did someone lend it to you?" asked Stephen. "Did you look at it in the library?" asked Stephen. "Did a teacher help you?" asked Stephen. "Did you get a contraband version?" asked Stephen.

Geoffrey's shoulders heaved with silent sobs.

"We won't stop with your finger," said Stephen. "Just tell us how you did it."

Geoffrey stood, head down, crying.

"Tell me!" Stephen suddenly shouted.

Shinty flinched. Geoffrey lunged forward and grabbed Stephen's habit, sending them both stumbling. Geoffrey was pushing, holding tight to the fabric, and screaming. "I didn't!" he screamed. "Fucking!" he screamed. "Do it!" he screamed. They collapsed in a heap, rolling through the garden beds. The other students slowly approached as the two struggled. Max and Lulu reached into the fray and grabbed Geoffrey, pulling him back, and tossing him onto the ground. Stephen scrambled to his feet. The back of his habit was covered in dirt and leaves. A blood smear was on the front.

"You fucking psych-out!" he shouted at Geoffrey. He stormed at Geoffrey, who recoiled into a ball, expecting a kick. Stephen kept walking, to the door, and out. The others followed, except for Pency, who knelt down next to Geoffrey.

The two looked at each other for a moment.

"We weren't going to cut off your finger," said Pency, quietly. Geoffrey sniffed and rubbed his hand over his face. "We just wanted you to tell us," said Pency. "We're giving you the silent treatment." Geoffrey stared at him. "I'm sorry," Pency whispered. "Please, just tell me." Tears shone in his eyes.

But Geoffrey dropped his head, his face looking to the ground. Slowly, with careful precision, he shook his head twice.

Pency sighed, exhaling with his whole body. He stood, looked down at his friend, and walked away.

Geoffrey's left hand was stinging. He inspected it, found a gash on the side of his palm. It must have happened when he grabbed for Stephen. He scooped up a clump of dirt and clapped it over the wound. Rub some dirt on it. He'd read that in a book somewhere. Hadn't he? His shoulders shook with a single sob.

Officers Tyrick, Brighton, and Third walked through the grounds. They came across the gravel path that circled the school and all three looked first right, then left. "Which way?" asked Tyrick. They stared down either path again. Brighton looked at the ground.

"That way," he said, nodding toward the right hand side.

"Why?" asked Third.

"Against traffic," Brighton said, pointing at a faint footprint. "Maybe we'll meet someone."

Zeke and Lin saw the trio of officers at the same time. They each dropped the other's hand but didn't break stride. Soon the five converged and stopped.

"Hello," said Tyrick.

"Hello," said Zeke.

There was a pause.

"We're here for the plagiarism investigation," Tyrick said, finally.

"Yes," said Zeke. "Thank you."

There was another pause. Tyrick tried again. "The lead investigator is meeting with your principal and another professor."

Lin looked up with a raised eyebrow, but said nothing.

"Would you like to join us?" Zeke asked, gesturing down the path.

"Oh," said Tyrick. "I wouldn't want to interrupt."

"Nonsense," said Zeke. "We were merely discussing pedagogical techniques. It would be most welcome to converse with some new faces."

"In that case, we'd be delighted," said Tyrick.

"Good's shit, but this is painful," said Third. "I've been in torture interrogations that were less forced."

Zeke smiled. "I'm sorry. We don't get many visitors."

"That's fine for you," said Third. "Doesn't excuse this one."

He waved at Tyrick.

Zeke smiled wider. "Then we're lucky you're here. My name is Zeke, and this is Lin."

"Hm," said Third. "This," he pointed at Tyrick, "Articulate fellow is Officer Tyrick. This," he pointed at Brighton, "is Officer Brighton. He's the one you'll want to talk to for any pedagogical discussions. And I'm Officer Third."

Zeke and Lin both looked confused. "Third?" said Lin.

"It means tertius," said Third, staring at him. Zeke laughed as Lin's confusion deepened. "This way then?" asked Third, and began to walk. The group followed.

"You're a soldier," said Brighton. Lin didn't react as the others all turned to look at him. They continued walking. "Where'd you serve?" asked Brighton.

Lin shrugged. "All over."

"What branch, I mean."

Lin sighed. "All over."

"Oh," said Tyrick. "You get repped?" Lin didn't reply. "It's no big concern," said Tyrick. "I got repped."

"Eight times," said Lin.

"Fuck me," said Third.

"Do you know which professor the primary investigator was talking to?" Zeke asked.

"What?" asked Tyrick, distracted.

Zeke hadn't changed the topic because she already knew the details. She didn't know the details. There was hardly a personal detail or story among the entire faculty that everyone else didn't already know. But Lin was the exception. He was the newest staff member, but that wasn't the reason. He didn't offer any details, and whenever someone asked too much, he grew more distant. The Principal knew the most, from Lin's hiring file, but of course wouldn't share it, which no one would ask for anyway. But Zeke knew that no file could have captured what a first generation soldier who had been reprogrammed eight times had seen. He was the favorite of the students.

"Do you know which professor," Zeke began.

"Oh," Tyrick said, registering the question. "Um, what was it?" he looked at Brighton.

"Bol Win, I think?"

Lin muttered under his breath. He and Zeke looked at each other.

"What? Why?" asked Third.

"Don't be so negative," Zeke said, smiling at Lin. "Do you know why they brought in bol Win?" she asked, looking at Tyrick.

Tyrick looked sideways at the two professors. "It was to provide some background information on the school and the students."

"Ha," said Lin.

"What did I say about being negative?" Zeke said.

"What's the story?" asked Third.

"Your investigator is going to get a perspective on this school that is not shared by the rest of the faculty," said Lin.

"What perspective is that?" asked Tyrick.

Now both Zeke and Lin sighed. "Maybe we shouldn't," Zeke said.

"What do I care?" said Lin, smiling. "What are they going to do? Fire me?" Zeke giggled.

"Do you mind if we stop?" asked Tyrick. He had been at the front of the group and had to keep turning back to listen. He gestured to a large flat rock just off the path. The greenhouse was just in sight. It was a clear day, as it typically was in that season. Bright sunlight, little wind, which was fairly unusual. The professors were comfortable in their habits. The officers slightly less so in their grey uniforms. Zeke pitied them their heavy boots.

The five sat. Zeke, Lin, and Brighton on the large rock.

Tyrick and Third on smaller ones.

"How much do you know about the school?" asked Zeke.

"Not much," said Tyrick. "It's one of the institutions for the omega generation."

Lin scoffed and shook his head. "That was a ridiculous name for it."

Tyrick shrugged. "That's what they call it."

"Anything else," said Zeke.

"Your focus is on reading and writing," said Tyrick.

"Imagination," said Brighton.

"What?"

"Their focus is on imagination." He turned to Zeke and Lin. "Isn't that right?"

Zeke nodded. "Yes. Imagination, creativity, artistic expression. Through the medium of writing," she added, with a nod to Tyrick.

"And the other schools, institutions, focus on other mediums?" asked Tyrick.

Third looked bored, casting his eyes around the landscape.

"We don't really know," said Lin.

"Why not?" asked Brighton.

"The idea was that the schools be kept isolated and that their work be protected," said Lin. "So that it didn't affect the work of the other schools."

"How many other schools are there?" asked Brighton. Zeke and Lin both shrugged. "You don't know?" Zeke shook her head. "Do you know if they're still in operation?" Zeke shook her head again.

"I think the Principal knows," she said. "And bol Win probably has an idea. They've been here since the beginning."

"Are they," Brighton hesitated.

"Yes," said Zeke. "First rounders. Bol Win might be the oldest person you'll ever meet."

Third sighed and stood up, stretching his legs restlessly.

"Is that where his particular perspective comes from?" asked Tyrick.

"What's going on over there?" asked Third. He had taken several steps in a circle, and was now facing the greenhouse. The other four turned to look.

"What is going on over there?" Lin repeated, putting emphasis on the second word. Students were walking out of the greenhouse and congregating in a group. They hadn't noticed the five adults, who were some distance off. "They should all be at chores. Is that all of them?"

"I don't see Geoffrey," said Zeke.

Third stared at the small mass of children all in identical habits and closely cropped hair. "You can tell who's who?"

"Yes," said Lin, simply. "And you're right. He's not there."

Tyrick grimaced as Zeke and Lin started walking toward the greenhouse.

Outside the greenhouse, Pency approached the students who stood in a group. "It doesn't make any sense," Lulu was saying.

"Why's he doing this?" asked Max.

They stood there, dejected. Pency raised his head. "What if he's protecting somebody?"

"What do you mean?" asked Lulu.

"Who would he be protecting?" asked Greta.

Pency exhaled sharply and wiped his hand over his face. He didn't know. None of it made any sense. Why was Geoffrey behaving this way? Why was Pency treating his friend this way? There needed to be a reason. If he could just figure it out.

"Look, why wouldn't he tell us?" asked Pency. "We know why he wouldn't tell the professors. He doesn't want to get expelled." Pency looked at each of them. "But why not us?

We're his friends."

"We were his friends," said Stephen, emphasizing the second word.

Pency turned on him. They were the two tallest students and were just about eye to eye. "Shut your mouth," Pency said, softly. "Your fucking scare tactic didn't work so you can just shut up from here on." Stephen stared at Pency sharply, then looked away. "Something else is going on," said Pency, emphatically. "There is a reason."

"You think he's protecting a professor?" asked Greta.

"He's got some kind of secret," said Pency. "What else could it be?"

"What's the secret?" asked Max.

Stephen suddenly raised his head and looked at Pency. "What if someone's really got a book."

Each child took a breath and drew their head back slightly, all at once. The air around them grew heavier and charged. Pency stared back at Stephen. "What if someone's got a library."

"Ssst!" Shinty hissed. "East, Greta and Wint."

Mart turned and headed directly to the greenhouse. Max and Lulu toward the school and an outer door. Stephen and Shinty walked west to connect with the path. Pency waited a beat then followed Max and Lulu. Greta and Wint began walking east to the path. They quickly came across Zeke and Lin.

"Students," said Zeke, skeptically.

"Hello, Professor Zeke," said Greta and Wint together. "Hello, Professor Lin." Both children nodded once.

Zeke looked down at the two. It was always them. "What are you all doing out here?"

"Playing catch-em-up," said Greta.

"Who are they?" Wint asked suddenly, looking past them. Zeke turned and saw the three officers sitting on the large rock, watching them. She sighed.

"They're here for the plagiarism investigation," she said, turning back to the children. "You will meet them later."

"They're on our way," said Wint.

"Go the other way," said Lin. "Get back inside, you little demons." He turned them around with a hand on each shoulder.

"But our chores are that way!" insisted Greta.

"And you can take the long way as punishment. You should be doing them right now, not playing games," said Lin.

"No one else is being punished," said Greta as they began walking.

"No one else got caught. Come on. Tell me a story with no adjectives. Swap sentences."

The three continued toward the school. Zeke made for the greenhouse with the sound of the exercise fading in her ears.

"There was a lake," started Greta.

"It was... there was no movement on the surface."

"All around were... trees and lilacs."

Zeke entered the greenhouse. Mart was watering while Geoffrey pruned. Both looked over at her and nodded, then resumed their tasks.

"Geoffrey," said Zeke. Geoffrey looked up.

"Yes, Professor Zeke?"

"What were you doing outside just now?" she asked.

"Playing catch-em-up," he said.

Had there been a hesitation there? Just the slightest hiccup? Zeke pursed her lips. "You're a mess," she said, noticing his habit. Geoffrey looked down at the dirt stains.

"I tripped," he said. "Sorry."

"No need to," Zeke started to say. "What happened to your hand?"

Geoffrey looked down again. His hand was caked in mud

but a bit of blood was seeping through. "I cut it," he said, too quickly he realized. "When I fell," he said, slower.

Zeke took his hand gently, but he winced. She carefully tried to examine it, but couldn't get past the dirt. "Why didn't you get it treated?" she asked.

"I - ouch!" he exclaimed. It was a good stall for a moment. "Didn't realize it was that bad," he finished. "It'll heal."

Zeke flaked some of the dirt off and saw the gash. "Not for a few days. And it will get infected." She looked up at Geoffrey who met her eyes. His eyes were a little too wide and his breathing a little too heavy. And he held eye contact for too long. Zeke sighed deeply. She felt like she would never understand their world. She had a hard time believing that there was a time when she could have. "Come on," she said. "Let's get you fixed up." The two walked out of the greenhouse, Mart watching. "You know," said Zeke. "Students under investigation shouldn't make it a habit to lie to their teachers."

"No indeed," said Geoffrey.

Third watched Zeke leading a child back to the school. He turned to the others. "Did you see them scatter like that? That was brilliant."

"And sending the two to intercept the teachers," said Brighton. "Wonderful tactics."

Tyrick kicked at the dusty ground and leaned back on the rock. Looking up at the sky, he had to squint from the bright.

"Do you think it was anything critical?" asked Brighton.

"Doubt it," said Third. "Probably just kids with their super secret kid stuff. That's what kids do, right?"

Brighton shrugged. "Your guess is as good as mine. They've had plenty of time to practice their spy craft anyway," he said. "Not much else to do around here." The three were quiet for a moment. "I bet they know what really happened," said Brighton. "Place like this? They know way more than the teachers."

Third laughed. "Yeah. They've probably been in every corner of this place."

"What do you think, boss?" asked Brighton, looking at Tyrick, still leaning back with his head lifted. His eyes had closed while the other two talked.

Tyrick was silent for several beats. "I think," he said, finally. "This place is unnatural. I think I would have liked to hear more about Professor bol Win. I think I'm tired. And I think there's not much reason for us to be here. But let's assist however we can, so we can get off this rock as soon as possible and get home."

Brighton and Third muttered agreement.

"How do we help?" asked Brighton.

Tyrick opened his eyes and looked at the two. "She'll start with information-gathering," he said. "Let her do her thing there, don't get in her way. Meantime, we'll collect as much intel as we can. Informally. Since we're really just along for the ride, let's use that to distance ourselves from the Investigator. If they don't think we're interrogating them, they might open up more. And they can't get many visitors, so they're likely to be talky. Everything we collect, we take back to her. The more information she has, the sooner she'll figure out all the pieces."

Brighton and Third nodded. "And then we get off this rock and go home?" asked Third, a touch too sarcastically.

Tyrick cocked his head. "This rock is home, isn't it?" he said.

Third nodded, solemnly. "Afraid so."

"Sure doesn't feel like it. Come on," Tyrick said, standing. "Let's verify the sat imagery and the blueprints as much as we can."

The three men continued on the path, their footfalls

raising small clouds of dust that clung to the hems of their pants and streaked boots. Over the horizon the sun was beginning to set, casting the world in orange. For a moment, caught between the burnt sky and the red dust creeping up his uniform, Tyrick felt like he was being devoured by a great monster swallowing them all up and in a moment there would be no trace of the three grey officers.

The Investigator sat, staring out the window. It was finally getting dark. Rocks stretched into eerie shadows and the light glowed like fire. What a strange place this was. The Principal had been chatting briefly with bol Win and Arden at the door, but now closed it and walked back to his desk. Passing the Investigator, he noticed the orange glow from outside was reflected in her eyes. It had been a long day for her, he knew. Who knew how long she'd been awake. The travel, arriving in a new place, processing all the new information, listening to bol Win drone on and on. That had been a mistake.

"I'm sorry," the Principal said, sitting down.

"Hm?" the Investigator came out of her trance.

"He can be," the Principal paused. "A bit tiresome. That was probably a great deal of useless information."

The Investigator smiled. "Oh," she said. "In most cases, about ninety-five percent of all the information I collect is useless. The problem is I have never figured out how to identify that five percent until the case is over." The Principal chuckled with her. The Investigator turned and looked back out the window. It was oddly soothing. And it had been a long day.

"No notes?" asked the Principal.

"I'll record them before I sleep," she said. "I've got a decent memory. Until I fall asleep."

"I know what you mean," the Principal said. "Sometimes I feel like I die every night and a new version of me starts the next day." The Investigator turned, a bit startled. It was a fairly odd remark to a person recently met. But the Principal paid little mind. "Like you're only really alive for one day," he said, staring off at his desk. "And then you're replaced by someone else with all your memories." He smiled and shrugged. "How would you know?"

The Investigator looked at the kindly man with white hair in front of her.

"When I was a child," she said. "I had a babysitter who would ride me around on their scoot-scoot."

"Their what?"

"Scoot-scoot? Two wheels, pedals."

"A bicycle?"

"Similar, but with a coil engine."

The Principal nodded.

"We'd ride around, me on the back holding on, just loving it. I grew up in a fairly deserted place. We could get out to some remote areas. Once, we had a nasty accident. I just remember the tires slipping and then I was going end over end. My sitter was knocked unconscious, and I couldn't wake her. I was so scared. And I had a broken arm. There was nobody in sight."

The Principal listened intently.

"The scoot was a mess, and I had no idea what to do. But I knew I had to get help for my sitter. Her name was Batten. So I started running. It ended up being seven or eight kilometers. With the broken arm too. I was a terrible mess before I finally came across a station."

"How old?" the Principal asked.

"Me? Nine. We got help for Batten. She was totally fine. And I even got a little medal for it from the local constable. I was so proud."

She stopped talking and stared out the window. The Principal waited. He looked at her face. It was calm. No clenched jaw. No furrowed brow. Everything about her exuded calm. Everything except her pale eyes. They flickered this way and that, alighting on a hundred different things in her field of vision. The Principal waited.

"That's the last clear memory I have of childhood. And it feels like it happened to a stranger. I don't recognize that child. When I think of it, when I tell that story, I'm so proud of that little girl, and I'm," she paused, searching. "Just pleased, I guess, that I can say I was that little girl. But it feels like a lie. It feels like she was part of a story you hear someone else tell about themselves. It feels," she stopped again, and her eyes glistened. "It feels like that little girl is dead. And that makes me very sad. I miss her."

Her hand came up and dashed across her eyes quickly. "Isn't that strange?" she said quietly. "I wonder sometimes how much of that memory is even real. How much has been distorted. And I suppose at some point, even that will be gone. Faded away. Makes me wonder if we're even prolonging our lives, or just replacing them. Like you said. A new version everyday. Sorry," she said, laughing a little. "You just reminded me of that moment." It had felt oddly comforting to tell the story.

Now the Principal looked down, staring again at his desk. The two sat in silence. Out the window, stars were slowly materializing in the pale sky. The Principal sighed and rubbed his hands on his desk. "I have no more memories of my childhood," he said. "Just feelings anymore. Just a sense of things."

The Investigator turned to look at him. "What feelings?"

The Principal closed his eyes, trying to shut out everything as he brought his mind backward in time. A colossal amount of time. An unnatural amount of time. "I remember it was hot," he said, still with his eyes tightly shut. "I remember being hungry. And I remember fear."

"Fear? Of what?"

The Principal opened his eyes and shrugged. "I can tell you what was going on in the world, because I've read about it, seen video clips, played the holo sequence. I've even got a bio-vid for more specifics of my own life. I know in great detail what happened in my life. But," he shrugged. "It's not in my memory. Like it happened to a stranger." He nodded to her. "Like your little girl." They were both quiet.

"Thank you," the Investigator said after a moment.

"For what?"

"For the conversation."

"Oh," the Principal waved his hand. "The thanks are mine. Talking to a new face is a rare treat. I fear my social skills are lacking."

The Investigator laughed. "In fact, it's quite nice to chat with someone who isn't obeying all the social mores." Now the Principal laughed. "I would like to speak further on your own perspective of the school though," the Investigator said. "I gather you differ somewhat from the good Professor bol Win." The Principal raised an amused eyebrow. "However," the Investigator said. "I am quite tired."

"Of course," said the Principal. "Tomorrow." He stood and extended a hand to the door. "I can show you to your room. Your officers?" he trailed off.

"I'll track them down."

"Yes, very good," said the Principal. "And all your beds are together."

A short time and a brief walk later, the Principal gestured into the spare room. Bunk beds lined the walls, three units on either side.

"Here you are," he said. "Will this suit?" The Investigator nodded, scanning the room. "Wash room is at the end of the hall," said the Principal, pointing. "You'll have to share, I'm afraid, but only with each other. The students and other faculty quarters are on different levels."

The Investigator nodded again. "We couldn't ask for more," she said, as the Principal surveyed the room. "Thank you. And thank you for your hospitality."

The Principal murmured, and headed down the hall.

Geoffrey sat on his bunk, trying not to look into the corner. That's where they all were. Talking. The sign language they had come up with was a way to communicate without the professors knowing what was going on. Now it was being used against him.

One day, quite a while ago, they had been on an excursion with Professor Lin, studying the geology of the half-bowl their school sat in, learning the story of the land. Professor Lin had packed a lunch for all of them, and everyone was sitting in a circle. All the students were signing, so that Professor Lin wouldn't know what they were talking about.

What had they even been talking about? Geoffrey tried to think back. It was something about the dirt, but he couldn't remember what. All he remembered now was seeing Professor Lin's face.

They all thought they were being sneaky, but he saw it. Geoffrey had glanced at him once, and it was clear as daylight on his face. He saw the conversation going on, but couldn't understand it. He had looked sad, Geoffrey thought. Dejected. He just wanted to be let in on what they were talking about. Just wanted to be a participant. Geoffrey had wanted to say something to him, out loud, so he could be included. But he didn't.

Now here he was.

But this was different, he thought. Professor Lin was a professor. He was an adult. He had other adults to talk to. They had their own conversations that the students weren't a part of. What did he have now? He couldn't be included in the professor's conversations, and he couldn't be included in the student's conversations. How long was this going to last? It couldn't last that long. Geoffrey glanced sideways at the corner. Pency was talking a lot. Seemed that way, anyway. His shoulders were moving. That had to be a good sign. Pency would stick up for him.

Geoffrey sighed and collapsed back on his bed. He had gone whole days before without speaking to anyone while working on a story. This could be a good time. He could write and think. A lot of good ideas could come from this. He sighed again. He hoped Pency could help.

There was rustling from the corner as the group disbanded and students made for their bunks. Geoffrey sat up, hopefully. Pency walked past and climbed into his bunk. He hadn't even looked at Geoffrey.

The last light was fading from the window. They were up late. Geoffrey lay back down and stared up at the ceiling. Tomorrow would be better.

FOUR

THE BOOK

"Can you tell me about the chemical signature?" she asked. The Principal gritted his teeth. She already knew all this. Nalin would play along though. The three were in a small room, standing around a book on a small table.

"Each book is given a marker, if you will," said Nalin, easily slipping into the role of lecturer. "It secretes this, obviously at a slow rate, but enough to leave a trace wherever it goes. This was put into place fairly early on, in order to discourage undermarket transactions. The value of our books is quite immense and we needed a way to track them over long periods of time and space."

"Do the books ever stop secreting this chemical?"

"Eventually they would, but..." Professor Nalin paused. "Not for ages."

"Has this limit been reached yet?"

"No," she said, with confidence.

"Thank you," the Investigator said. "If you could give us a few minutes." Professor Nalin nodded and exited.

"You knew all that," said the Principal.

The Investigator nodded while turning the book over in her hands. "Just confirming."

"And you've already scanned the area?"

"When we were docked." She glanced up at the Principal who had raised an eyebrow. "We didn't find anything. Is this the only copy?" asked the Investigator, staring down at the closed book.

"No," said the Principal. "There's one on the Dante, and another in the Central Authority library in Brighton, South

America." The Investigator looked up. "Is Officer Brighton from Brighton?" asked the Principal.

The Investigator stared at him. "No," she said, finally. "I mean, is this the only copy at the school?"

"Ah," said the Principal. "Yes."

The Investigator smiled and returned to the book. It was face up. In bold, raised letters on the cover was the title and the author. The cover was gray and soft. She ran her finger along the edge. Carefully, she lifted the cover with one finger. The Principal watched with a concerned look on his face.

"It's not going to break," he said. The Investigator looked up again, lowering the cover. "The book," said the Principal. "It's not going to break. They're highly durable."

The Investigator laughed sheepishly. "It's just..." she hesitated. "It's strange to think that there are so few."

"Mm," said the Principal. "Yes." He looked down at it, laying on the table. "Well, that's why they're so durable." And smiled.

The Investigator smiled too, and opened the book. The handwritten words danced in front of her eyes. It was like a jumble that slowly fell into place as her mind remembered the pieces. When was the last time she had held a book? She moved her hand over a page. She'd opened randomly, almost halfway. Everything in perfect lines across each page. "Wonderful," she murmured. She suddenly turned to the last page, the words ending neatly halfway down, and looked up. "How do you know how many pages you'll need?" she asked.

"We know from the original copy," said the Principal.

"But how can you be sure you'll match it? There must be some variations in the copying." The Principal shrugged slightly. The Investigator's eyes widened and she dropped her chin. "You can be that precise?"

"We've had a lot of practice," the Principal said, playfully.

The Investigator looked back down, then again at the

Principal. "It's very impressive work," she said simply.

"Thank you," the Principal nodded in appreciation. "Although, Professor Arden should take the credit for that. He instructs everyone in handwriting."

"The students?"

"No," said the Principal. "I mean, yes, but not just the students. Also all the professors. To even out all our individual quirks and get as uniform a text as possible. That allows for the precision."

"Who wrote this?" asked the Investigator, returning to the book.

"Sheridan Le Fanu," the Principal said politely.

The Investigator smiled. "No. Who copied it?"

"Of course," said the Principal, embarrassed. "It's on the title page. At the beginning," he added.

The Investigator flipped to the front. It took a moment for the name to register. She'd gotten used to thinking of him as his title. "You wrote this?"

"I merely copied it." But he blushed slightly.

The Investigator hefted the book. It felt strangely satisfying. The cover was soft, but with an interesting texture and firmness. The pages were thin and the book could be bent slightly in a pleasing way. "And the other copies?" she asked. "The ones on the Dante and at the Central Library?"

"Also mine. We tend to have the same person write multiple copies. It goes a little faster, we've found," the Principal said.

"It feels nice," the Investigator said, bending the book. "Doesn't it?" The Principal smiled and murmured agreement. "Do you make the books here? The blanks, I mean?"

"Oh, no," said the Principal. "They're made at a zero gee station and dropped down every so often, so to speak," the Principal smiled at his own joke.

The Investigator continued. "And Nalin's analysis revealed

that the boy had never touched it, or just hadn't touched it recently?"

"Almost certainly never," said the Principal.

"How sure can you be?"

"It's been handled quite infrequently and kept in a sealed state in our library," said the Principal. "We can tell whenever anyone has touched it at all and we can match trace DNA elements of someone to the person. We have a very high degree of confidence to tell you every single person who has ever touched that book." The Principal stopped and looked down. He squeezed his eyes shut tight and pressed his fingers to his temples. This wasn't right. What was he doing? This was exactly what he wanted to avoid and here he was again. It was so easy to fall into this trap.

"Something wrong," asked the Investigator.

The Principal shook his head slowly, as if to clear it. "It's..." he paused. "Just..." he paused again. "This was all in our report. You know the answers to these questions. You must have asked questions to people like this thousands of times." He looked up at the Investigator. "What are we even doing here? What is the point of this exchange of information that you already have?" The Principal stepped back suddenly. His eyes moved almost frantically around the room, seeing nothing. "It's all the same. It's all the same story, the same..." H shook his head again, quickly this time, as if to dash away the thoughts inside it. "Same, same everything. What's new?" His hands hung at his sides now. They felt useless, like he should be doing something with them but he didn't know what. He stopped talking, stopped moving, merely hung his head.

The Investigator watched him. Throughout, her face had transitioned from slight surprise to concern to finally calm. An almost imperceptible downward turn of her eyes and the slightest crease on her forehead gave away the delicate feeling of sadness. "I'm sorry," she said.

The Principal waved his hand. "You're sorry?" he said, feeling ridiculous with himself. "I'm the one."

"I am," the Investigator interrupted. "I know you don't like this kind of talk. You said so yesterday." She shrugged. "It's hard to get away from it. It's a habit."

The Principal gave a short laugh, and pulled at his own habit. "I'm sorry," he said, emphasizing the first word. "I don't know what came over me."

The Investigator smiled. "We don't need another rote conversation," she said.

The Principal barked a laugh again. "Thank you," he said. "Doesn't it get tiring though, asking questions you already know the answers to?"

"I'm trying to get more answers," she said. "About the situation, the people, the person I'm talking to. The same story can be told by two different people in two very different ways."

"Mm," the Principal nodded. "That's true."

"Often the reports I receive are riddled with errors or gaps." The Principal looked up sharply. "Yours was uncommonly good," the Investigator reassured him. The Principal nodded in satisfaction. "But there are always new pieces of information to gather," said the Investigator. "Otherwise, why would I even be here. Like my discussion with bol Win. The two of you don't share the same opinion of this..." she paused. "Experiment."

The Principal's eyes sharpened, just for a moment. But the Investigator had caught the flash across his face. That had been the wrong word.

"This is not an experiment," the Principal said, slowly but firmly. "This..." he stopped and the flash came back over his face. The Investigator saw his cheeks ripple as the jaw muscles worked. "These are their lives," he hissed, staring directly at the Investigator. She waited, holding the intense gaze. "They're in prisons!" he flailed his arm helplessly. "Prisons we made for crimes we committed." His eyes glistened. The Principal turned away. The Investigator held her breath.

It was very quiet. The room they were in was small. There was a table, which currently held the school's only copy of Carmilla, by Sheridan Le Fanu. There was a chair but it had been pushed up against the wall. There were no windows, only a single door, which led back to the library. The Investigator wondered if it was soundproof. It probably was.

"Bol Win thinks this is some noble venture," the Principal grimaced. "He thinks this is right." He turned back to the Investigator.

"And you don't?"

The Principal's upper lip actually curled back, as though he were snarling, the Investigator thought. "Although I'm quite sure the answer to that question was not in your report," the Principal said. "I'm also quite sure you already know the answer to it." He stared at the Investigator. "Please stop asking me questions you already know the answer to."

The Investigator nodded once. "Okay," she said. "Do you disagree with this mission enough to sabotage it?"

The Principal sighed and nodded to himself. That was a fair question. "I disagree, vehemently, with what was done to these children," he said. "But I would not sabotage what we're doing here. And I certainly wouldn't twist one of my students around like a pawn."

"If there is success here," the Investigator said. "Might it lead to another round of subjects?"

The Principal raised an eyebrow at the word subjects. The Investigator held his look. After a moment, the Principal scoffed. "Success," he said. "What does success even look like? You called this an experiment? Experiments have ends.

How long have we been down here, trying to do what? Provide some new spark of creativity for humanity." The Principal sighed. "What a ridiculous idea," he said, softly. The Investigator waited. "You know," the Principal said, after a moment. "It's easy to get into the routine of teaching and caring for these kids. The day-to-day tasks allow you to forget about..." He raised his hands. "The bigger picture. Which is lucky, because if I dwelt on our mission, I'd probably never get out of bed. Sabotage this mission? This experiment? There's nothing to sabotage. All I care about is making sure these children are tended to properly." The Investigator nodded in acceptance. "Besides," the Principal added. "There's no stomach for another round of..." he paused. "... subjects." He smiled. "Thank mercy for that."

"Well," the Investigator said. She had been in this strange little room long enough. The recycled air reminded her too much of a ship. "Let's get out of here." She tapped the book. "There's nothing here I don't already know from your report," she said, smiling.

The Principal laughed. "I flew off the handle, didn't I? I don't feel myself these days," he rubbed his face.

"Stress, I suppose," said the Investigator. The two headed for the door and continued out. "Although I can't imagine why."

The Investigator walked back to the shared room. As she entered, Tyrick and Third were playing cards. "Where's Brighton?" she asked.

Tyrick nodded his head to her. "Chief," he said. "He's finishing up in the washroom."

"Sevens," said Third.

The Investigator sighed and sat down. She pulled her tablet from a side pocket on her pants and stared down at the blank screen.

"Eights," said Third.

"Analyze conversation subject two past forty minutes. Analyze evidence item one historical," the Investigator said. The screen came alive. A video of the past forty minutes, as seen from her eyes, flashed quickly by. Images of the book blinked past next.

"Nines," said Third.

"Anything we should know?" asked Tyrick.

Third grabbed Tyrick's wrist and stared directly at him. "I'm your father," Third said. Tyrick shook his hand free.

The Investigator continued to watch the screen as the data readout appeared. "Psychology," she said.

Third turned over his shoulder to look at her. "Is he all there?" he asked.

Brighton walked in scratching his head. "Is who all there?" he asked. Then, noticing the Investigator, he nodded and said, "Chief."

"The Principal," said Third.

"The boy?" asked Brighton.

"Not the principal, you idiot. The Principal."

Brighton looked down over Tyrick's shoulder at the cards he was holding. Brighton held up four fingers to Third.

"Fours," said Third.

"Tens," said Tyrick, dropping three cards.

"What?" Third said. Brighton laughed. "We're betting on this!" Third yelled at him.

"You shouldn't cheat," said Brighton. He walked to his bunk and began pulling clothes from a bag. "How long do you think we'll be here?" he asked.

"Long enough for me to win back my pride," said Third.

"Forever then," said Tyrick.

"Sevens," said Third.

"You just said that."

"I'm saying it again."

The Investigator looked up at the three of them. She blinked and a quizzical expression crossed her face. There was Brighton, standing at his bunk, going through his things. There were Tyrick and Third, playing cards and ribbing each other. And here she was, going over the investigatory analysis. How many times had this happened? How many times in how many corners of the galaxy they had been in a place just like this? She blinked again. Brighton's hair was slightly damp. Tyrick was in short sleeves, which meant the scar on his left forearm was visible. Third was holding his cards the way he always did, all in a stack, kept close to his chest. The windows were bright with sunlight, but it wasn't coming directly in, and it was tinted. The ceiling was a filament cover, which was currently set at around fifty percent she guessed.

"Chief?"

"Hm?" she turned to Tyrick, who was looking at her, concerned.

"You okay?"

"Yeah," she shook her head. "Just..." she paused. "Laggy."

Third grunted. "Tell me about it," he said. "Starving too."

Tyrick kept looking at the Investigator. "Anything we should know about?" he asked again. She absentmindedly shook her head.

"How's the investigation going?" Third asked, arching his eyebrows and with an edge to the question.

The Investigator looked back down at the screen, bringing herself back from the daze. "The Principal's suspect rating is less than one," she brushed her fingers over the screen. "I'm overriding that to zero. He's a nice man. Stressed," she said. "Maybe going through a midlife crisis." The three officers laughed. "The book is..." she paused. "A book. Nothing new. Their analysis is better than ours and the process was confirmed solid."

"Wait, are we treating this like a real investigation?" asked

Third.

"Who did the analysis?" asked Tyrick.

"Subject eight. Nalin," said the Investigator.

"Does that mean he's off the hook?" asked Tyrick.

The Investigator shrugged. "She. And no," she said. "I want motive and that's the biggest information deficit right now. I'll be talking to subject one after lunch. With any luck, he'll tell me who helped him."

"Any chance it was a solo job?"

"Very unlikely," she said. "It's at twenty percent at the moment but that will be adjusted after the interview. But I can't imagine he did this alone." She looked up from the tablet. "You're all very welcome, by the way," she said. "I didn't force you to listen to that bol Win. Five minutes in and I felt like I was in a training seminar."

Tyrick laughed. "I was sorry to miss out on that," he said. "Anything useful though?"

She shook her head. "Just that he thinks this is all very noble," she said. "He didn't say it but that's the impression. He thinks they're doing great things here."

Brighton scoffed. "Torturing kids is pretty noble, isn't it?"

"Who's torturing kids?" said Third.

"Officer Tyrick," said the Investigator. "Please ensure that all your direct reports carefully study the case files prior to the commencement of the investigations."

"What for?" Third grumbled. "I'm about as useful here as Tyrick is at cards."

Tyrick stared down at the table. "I'm beating you!" he protested.

"What do you want me to do?" Third continued. "Strong arm one of these kids? Or the teachers? I can do all kinds of damage to that fossil you were talking to yesterday." A chime sounded throughout the room. "Lunch!" Third said, standing.

"Just try to behave," the Investigator said.

The four walked into the dining area. It was a large room with a high ceiling. Round tables were scattered about. Students and teachers filled the area, most already seated. Each table only had five chairs, but even so there were more than enough seats. At the far end of the room were steaming trays laid out in a row on a long table. Third started directly toward them, Brighton and Tyrick not far behind. Students quieted and stared at the new faces. The teachers tried to act casually but the Investigator saw the looks and the forced conversations.

"Welcome," a voice beside her said. She turned and saw the Principal seated with Professor Arden. "Will you join us?" asked the Principal.

"Thank you," said the Investigator, looking around the room. "I feel a bit out of place."

The Principal waved his hand and stood up. "Oh, never mind that," he said. "We'll introduce you to everyone after the meal." He gestured to a seat. "Please. I'll bring food." And he walked away.

The Investigator stepped around the table and took a seat with her back to the wall. Arden nodded in greeting. "The Principal was just telling me about your talk this morning," Arden said. He waited a moment. "He was a little embarrassed," he said, after the Investigator made no sign of responding. Now she shrugged.

"Nothing to be embarrassed about," she said.

"He said he's not really feeling himself."

"What's for lunch?" asked the Investigator.

Arden hesitated for a moment at the topic change. Then he flourished his hand over his plate. "Rice, vegetables, tofu," he said. "Actually there should be bread as well," he added. "He should bring you some." The Investigator murmured appreciatively. "He didn't really go into specifics though,"

Arden said. There was another pause. "About the conversation the two of you had." The Investigator looked around the room.

"Is this everyone from the school?" she asked.

Arden gritted his teeth and glanced over the dining area. "Yes," he said, curtly.

"And how many students?" asked the Investigator.

"Nine."

Nine," the Investigator repeated. "I thought it was ten."

"It was ten," Arden said. "There was a transfer."

"A transfer?" she asked. "Is that common?"

Arden shrugged. "No," he said. "But it's not terribly uncommon. It happens. It wasn't the first time a student was transferred from an omega school."

"No?"

"Updated skills tests can prompt that kind of thing."

"When was that?" the Investigator asked.

"Oh," he frowned at the calculation. "Some time ago," he said, finally.

A tray of food clattered down, followed by Third. Tyrick and Brighton were close behind. "Bread!" Third said, offering a piece to the Investigator.

"Professor Arden," Tyrick said in greeting. Arden nodded back. "Did you serve?" Tyrick asked, noting Arden's skin tones.

"I didn't," Arden said. "My father did though. He was a navy marshal for the Arctic bloc."

"Thought you looked a little old for it," said Tyrick. "Got the genes though, eh?"

"Mm," Arden nodded. "And my mother was a pirate," he said. "No one's quite sure how I ended up as a professor."

The three officers laughed.

"That must be a good story," said the Investigator. "Romance on the high seas."

Arden smiled and shrugged. "It sounds more exciting than it actually is."

"Still," said the Investigator. "Have you written it out?"

Arden nodded. "I have, but..." he sighed. "Not terribly well, I must say." He moved some rice around on his plate. "I was hoping a student would be able to help me out with it at some point." He looked up at the officers. "You probably have your share of stories as well. Erinyes class, is it?"

Tyrick nodded. "It is," he said simply.

The Principal returned with a tray of food and set it in front of the Investigator before sitting down. "I hope that's alright," he said. "Gourds, peppers, and lettuce."

"Thank you," said the Investigator. "It looks wonderful. Professor Arden was telling us about a story he's working on."

"Oh?" said the Principal, returning to his own food. "Which one is that?"

"About my parents," said Arden.

"Ah yes!"

"It needs work," said Arden. "I was saying I was hoping a student could help."

"Yes, yes," said the Principal. He looked around the room. "I suppose we'll introduce you shortly," he said.

"But I thought the stories the officers could tell might be more interesting," Arden said carefully. "Especially considering their unit designation."

"I'm sorry, their what?" The Principal turned back to Arden, a confused expression knitted into his brow. The Investigator glanced at him. He seemed more distracted today.

"Their unit designation," Arden repeated. "The Erinyes."

"Oh!" The Principal's eyes brightened in recognition at the word. "I'm afraid I don't keep up with government classifications," he said. "But the Erinyes. Do you know the story?" Now he busied himself with his food. "The vengeful goddesses of old, the Furies." The Investigator smiled to herself. She knew the story, but he seemed to enjoy recounting it. She saw a muscle ripple in Arden's cheek though; that one had wanted the attention. "Born of Hell and the Night, they pursue sinners relentlessly, torturing them to death." The Principal chuckled. "Quite a grim namesake, no?" He looked up at the Investigator. "But there are four of you," he said, concerned.

"I'm not part of the group," the Investigator said. "So it's still an appropriate triptych."

The Principal smiled. "Still though," he said. "Grim."

"Central Authority does still enjoy a flair for the dramatic in their naming conventions," Arden said. "And they still pursue new weapon variants, don't they?" The Investigator saw his eyes flicker over Brighton and Third, but they were both ignoring him.

Tyrick, however, was not. "You keep up on the developments?" he asked.

Arden shrugged. "As I can. It's helpful for contemporary stories. And for writing science fiction. Taking what currently exists and expanding outward."

"Mm," Tyrick returned to his food.

"Of course, it's hard to know everything that's in development. I'm sure they keep much of it top secret," Arden was trying to be casual. The Investigator shook her head slightly.

"Mm," Tyrick said again, without looking up.

"Well then," said the Principal. "Shall we do introductions?"

Eight students were in the courtyard. Max and Lulu pretended to play stones. It was all very exciting, wasn't it? They hadn't gotten to play this much cloak and dagger in ages. Maybe ever. It was terrible about Geoffrey. But still, what was really the worst that could happen? That Investigator and her officers would sort it out quickly. Probably. And it was a good game. Even if Stephen and Pency were taking it so seriously. Anyway, it was a nice day. They had extra free time. And it was a good game.

"This would be easier if we talked to Geoff," Pency said, again.

"Would you shut up with that?" said Wint. "You're not helping." Pency scowled at him.

"Wait a minute," said Stephen. "What if it helped?" Everyone looked at him in surprise. There was a silence.

"You're the one saying along we should keep up the silent treatment," said Wint.

"I know, shut up," said Stephen. "I've been thinking. What's more damaging to our mission?"

"Oh, fuck," muttered Pency, and turned away.

"What?" challenged Stephen.

"This mission bullshit."

"It's not bullshit!" Stephen stood with his feet set slightly apart and his hands clenched into fists at his sides. His body shook as he stared at Pency's back. Pency turned around. "It's not bullshit," Stephen repeated, lowering his voice to what he thought was a growl. "We are here to," he hesitated. "Save humanity. From," he hesitated again.

"From what?" asked Pency. "That's propaganda. We're not saving shit from shit." Stephen glared at Pency.

"What are you two idiots fighting for?" asked Wint. "You were just about to agree on talking to Geoffrey. Which is stupid."

"What's stupid?" asked Lulu. "Them agreeing or talking to Geoffrey?"

"What?" asked Wint. "Talking to Geoffrey."

"Oh. That wasn't clear."

"Are you kidding me right now?"

Lulu shrugged.

"Why is it stupid?" asked Stephen.

Wint looked stunned. He had not expected to have to repeat Stephen's own arguments back to him. Wint held out a fist and started counting off on his fingers. "He cheated. There have been no consequences."

Pency interrupted. "We don't know if he cheated."

Wint threw his hands up in the air. Max whistled once, loudly and sharply. "Fuck," Max whispered.

Third and Brighton were already well into the courtyard before Max had noticed them. Wint, Pence, and Stephen stood very still. Lulu moved a stone. Shinty nudged Greta.

"How," Greta said, then started over. "Do you want to trade chores?" She winced and shook her head. Shinty glared at Max.

The officers approached the group of children and stopped. "Hello," said Brighton. The children glanced at each other. Lulu moved another stone.

"Crickets," said Third. "Do you let the other fella take a turn?"

Lulu froze. Max spoke, too quickly. "We have different rules." That wasn't technically a lie. So he hadn't lied to the officers. No one could get him for that.

"Huh," said Third. He looked at Brighton and shrugged.

Brighton stared down at the group of children who were all doing their best to ignore him and Third. He'd never seen so many kids all together. Probably never would again after they cleared this assignment. They were all so alien. He felt very clumsy in this moment. These children were nervous, scared. He and Third were the powerful grown-ups. But he and Third were the youngest people in the courtyard.

"Have you ever seen an android?" asked Greta suddenly.

"Yup," Third nodded, and gestured at Brighton. "This one's an android, you know."

All the children stared in shock at Brighton. Brighton looked exasperated. "I'm not an android," he said. All the children looked disappointed. "Every android is on a spaceship," Brighton said. "Called the Virgil."

"We know about the Virgil," Greta said, unimpressed.

"Oh," said Brighton.

"But have you seen one?" Greta asked again.

"Yes, we have," Third said. "Honest," he said, when Greta squinted at him. "We've been at Base One when the Virgil has docked. The androids come aboard the station for a while then."

"Is it true that no humans are allowed on the Virgil?" asked Greta.

"That is true," said Third. "But Officer Tyrick, the other one of us, has been on board the Dante."

"Are there really holograms where it's like you're riding a dinosaur?" asked Shinty.

"Um, yes," Third looked confused. "In some places." The children murmured.

"What's the farthest you've ever been away from Earth?"

"Have you been to a different planet?"

"Of course they have, stupid."

"Do you have any pets?"

"What?" asked Third.

"Pets," repeated Greta.

"What were y'all arguing about when we walked up?" asked Brighton. The children froze again. The two officers waited. It was quiet and the sun was warm. Third looked around, taking in the surroundings, waiting. Brighton looked from one pair of downturned eyes to the next. He knew all the names but he'd have a time sorting out who was who. All buzzed heads and identical habits. There were some skin tone variations but not a lot of range there either. It was hard even to tell the boys from the girls. "So you know why we're here," said Brighton. None of the children responded. "Well," Brighton continued. "It sounded like you were arguing about your friend Geoffrey." Still silence. Brighton and Third looked at each other. They weren't about to start interrogating children. But it had looked like a fierce argument had been taking place.

"I have to say," Third said, squatting down and peering at the stones diagram. "Those were some excellent tactics you pulled yesterday outside the greenhouse." Now the children looked up at him, interested. "The dispersal, heading off the teachers. I bet you all had the same story too, right?" Stephen looked down quickly. "Oh, hey," said Third. "We're not trying to trip any of you up." He gave a back-handed wave to Brighton. "We're really just along for the ride here. We're not part of the investigation."

Now Stephen looked back up at him. "Horses," said Stepehen. The rest of the children gaped.

Third looked up at Brighton who looked as confused as Third. "Horses?" repeated Third.

Lulu bit her lip, then said softly. "It means you're lying."

"Oh?" Third said, smiling. He looked at Stephen who was staring directly back at him. "Horses," said Third. "I haven't heard that expression. Have you heard that?" he turned back to Brighton.

"I haven't," said Brighton. "I've heard of horse shit." The children giggled.

Third shrugged at Stephen. "It's true," he said. "We were with the Investigator for a different case and we got routed here with her before going home. Normally, we wouldn't be assigned to this kind of thing."

Stephen narrowed his eyes. "What was the other case about?"

"It was a theft," said Third.

"What was stolen?"

"Favors."

"How can you steal favors?"

"It's a type of currency."

"Who did it?"

Brighton interjected quickly. "Ongoing investigation," he said.

"What were you arguing about?" Third asked.

Stephen blinked, hesitated, then glanced around at the other students.

"We were arguing about Geoffrey," Pency said softly.

Third and Brighton both turned to Pency, a bit surprised. "Yeah?" said Brighton.

"Yeah," said Pency.

"What about Geoffrey?"

There was another short silence before Pency answered. "Whether or not he cheated."

"Mm," said Brighton. He hoped it sounded concerned but still friendly. How did you talk to kids? Was he being patronizing?

"You don't think he cheated," Third said, looking at Pency. Pency looked at the ground. Third nodded.

"He's the only one," said Stephen. "We all know he cheated."

"Okay," said Third. "So what if he did?"

Brighton watched the reactions play out across the group. It was startling. Obviously plagiarism was a serious offense, even more so given the setting. But it was as if Third had suggested ritual suicide. The taboo of the crime was extreme. It made sense, Brighton supposed. The idea of it had been built up and up in these perpetually developing minds. The girl - Brighton thought she was a girl - who had been playing stones actually fell backward. Her opponent had turned, mouth open and eyes wide. This was the most prevalent expression. But a couple had anger written on their faces, in addition to the shock of it. It had been a good play by Third.

"So what?" Stephen finally gasped. Even Pency looked stunned.

Third kept up the act. "Yeah. So what?"

"Are you stupid?" Stephen spluttered. Third smiled. "To take the words, the ideas! Of another person and pass them off as your own is," Stephen shook his head. "Your last case," he said. "Someone stole some money?" Third nodded. "Money can be replaced. Whatever it buys can be replaced. The person who got robbed can speak up and say what was wrong. You can't replace someone's thoughts," Stephen was talking louder and louder. "Sheridan Le Fanu isn't here to say that these are his words. Wars have been fought over ideas." He was going a little off the rails here, Third thought. Getting a bit scattered. The kid was quite upset. Third raised his hands.

"Just fooling," he said. There was audible relief from the children. The angry one still looked angry. It would take a moment for that to dissipate.

"Do you even know what we're doing here?"

"I said I was just fooling," Third repeated.

Stephen shook his head and walked a few steps away. His face was hot and his heart was beating loud and fast. He tried to slow his breathing. It had just been a joke. Or a test. Maybe they were trying to see if the students really were against plagiarism. That made sense. It was a test. And he had passed. Stephen's breathing calmed, and his heart wasn't so loud in his ears.

Third and Brighton shared a look with each other. These kids were nothing else if not committed.

Tyrick walked slowly down a hallway. He stopped at a room and peered inside. There was a large ring-shaped table taking up the majority of the room. Chairs were all around it.

Tyrick noticed a gap in the circular table, so someone could stand in the middle. He craned his head in, scanning the walls. Flat stone. A window on one side, narrow, tinted. It was a drab room. Rock and plastic. Probably. The table and chairs couldn't be wood, although they looked it. They would have disintegrated long ago. Unless they were treated. They used to do that.

Tyrick sighed.

How much time had these kids spent in this room? Or the whole school? It was interesting hearing the others talk about their childhoods. They could barely remember their lives before treatment. But not him.

Some days it felt like that's all he could remember. Training and training and training and conditioning. Learning tactics and theory. Learning the practice of war. The glory of it. Sadness came over his face.

What a waste. How many resources had been spent to turn so many lives into incinerated flesh and bone? The table reminded him of a sparring circle. He walked into the room, into the middle of the table, and closed his eyes.

Jermond. That had been the name of the boy. They would have been the same age as the children here. Fighting naked in a pit. A little smaller than this table. The instructors would match you with someone exactly your size. Same height, same weight. And then we would fight. To find those with inner strength, we were told.

Tyrick sat on the cold floor. Why couldn't he just forget this? Punishment, I suppose. That was fair. He saw that boy's face. There was something written on it. Like an invisible tattoo. It wasn't anything describable. No specific expression. No grimace or scowl. Nothing even in those flat eyes. But written there all the same, as Tyrick's hands tightened, was fear.

The trainees were supposed to yield if they were beaten

or stand back if their opponent was clearly beaten. Jermond hadn't yielded. The brainwashing they all received about never failing saw to that. And Tyrick hadn't stood back.

Officially, he was reprimanded. Unofficially, he was congratulated. The instructors celebrated him. They cheered his brutality. Tyrick opened his eyes.

That was long ago. Nothing to do now but remember. Remember so it would never happen again and remember as penance for his crimes. Too many killings since then to count and none stuck with him. Young Jermond was the price for all of it. Standing, Tyrick walked out of the room, his head down and his hands clasped behind his back.

The Investigator and the boy sat in the room. They were at a small table, facing each other. It was the same room where the Investigator had examined the book. Geoffrey had spent a long time in this room, and the others like it, poring over books, basking in faraway places. Fiction or non, they could only ever exist in his imagination. And he loved visiting them. Loved seeing how words carefully selected and properly ordered could transport him to new lands and meet new people. So Geoffrey loved this room. But now it was not so comforting.

The Investigator had a nice face, but he knew it didn't matter. She was out to get him. She would ask all the same questions, and wouldn't believe any of his answers, just like all the others. He stared back at her with a calm face. There was no defiance or anger, or even sadness, which she had seen from the interrogations conducted over her tenure. He just looked accepting. Just a little boy. The Investigator had never interviewed a child before. Not even as a victim or a witness. She certainly never expected to be treating one as a suspect.

She had all the questions she was going to ask. All ready to go back over every statement he had given. Looking for the slightest discrepancy. But he had been asked these questions so many times before, and never wavered. Either he was telling the truth, which was statistically so unlikely that it wasn't responsible to even consider it, or he had fully committed to his story. It was second nature to him now. This boy who told stories had come up with one for himself. And he had repeated it over and over so that there wasn't a flaw.

"Would you like some water?" the Investigator asked.

"No, thank you," said the boy.

What was the point of all the questions she was going to ask? To go over the same ground she already knew about? Getting answers she already had?

The door opened and Professor Zeke entered. She sat at a corner of the table, to Geoffrey's right. Zeke nodded to the Investigator, and smiled at Geoffrey.

"How do you think it happened?" the Investigator asked.

The boy looked confused. Professor Zeke did as well. The professor had been given the list of questions the Investigator had planned on asking. This wasn't on it.

"How did what happen?" asked the boy.

"Your story. How was it just like the other one?"

The boy frowned. "I don't know." The Investigator waited. "It just was," said the boy.

The Investigator nodded, then shrugged. "If you had to guess."

The boy started to look worried. He turned to Professor Zeke who, to her credit, didn't say anything to him. "Guess?"

"Yeah," said the Investigator. She pushed the tablet in front of her away. The preset questions on it were useless anyway. "Say, if you were writing a story. How would you have something like this happen?"

The boy blinked. But slowly the gears shifted. The Investigator saw it on his face. He went from wondering why the question was asked to how he might solve the problem.

"Maybe," he said. "It was just luck."

"Well," the Investigator sighed and wagged her head from side to side. "That's basically impossible. But it did happen. So how else could it have happened?"

The boy looked at the table, then back up. "You mean, like if I wasn't making up the story?"

"Sure."

"Could it be paranormal?"

"Sure," said the Investigator. "Just brainstorm some ideas."

The boy's eyes narrowed. "Like osmosis?" he said. "Or maybe some kind of thought control." The Investigator waited. "Or past lives!" the boy said.

"Past lives?"

"Yeah!" said the boy. "Like I'm the reincarnation of that guy." He was sitting up straighter and his hands had moved from under his legs to on to the table.

"Okay. Past lives. I like that one."

"Yeah!" the boy repeated.

Professor Zeke had an expression of confusion and amusement, but still said nothing.

"I'm not so sure about osmosis though," said the Investigator.

"Yeah, that's stupid."

"How do you think thought control would work?"

"It'd be like," the boy's eyes squinted again in thought. "Concentrated sound waves making tiny vibrations in your head and making you do stuff."

"Like a radio transmission?"

"Yeah!" the boy's eyes now lit up. "Do they still have those?"

"They do, in some places."

"But super concentrated. Like a laser. Like what they use for FTL communication. But it's tuned to affect synapses in your head."

"So is it controlling actions or just suggesting them?"

"It's controlling," said the boy. "But what about subliminal messages. Would that work?"

The Investigator shrugged. "What do you think?"

The boy frowned. "No," he said. "It would have to be really precise for the copy to be exact." He thought for a moment. "I don't think the past lives thing works either."

"Why not?"

"Because you never write the same thing twice," said the boy. "You know if you lose something and you have to try to write it down again? It's never the same."

The Investigator nodded, not relating to the example in the slighest.

"An exact copy is too precise," said the boy. "And there's editing and everything. It'd have to be someone controlling your brain."

"With the radio transmission?"

"Yeah. Or what if someone memorized it perfectly, and then took over your body?"

The Investigator looked confused. "Isn't that like thought control?"

"No. Kind of," said the boy. "Like they were possessing you. All the way in your head. Not just messing with a machine that did it."

"Okay."

"Is there anything that can do that?"

The Investigator frowned. "Not without a lot of sensors attached to the person being controlled."

"Maybe it's a new invention," said the boy.

"Maybe," said the Investigator. She looked at the boy. His eyes were scanning back and forth on the table, imagining different scenarios, working out problems. She hated to break him out of his little reprieve. "Do you think," she said gently. "One of those reasons is what happened to you?"

"Huh?"

The Investigator watched him carefully. She saw the fantasy fall away and get replaced with the remembered reality. Saw how crushing that was for him. One moment, he was plotting a science fiction adventure, and the next he was back in this little room in the real world. The realization of why he was here came crashing back down on him.

"Do you think that's what happened to you?" she asked again.

He shrugged, miserable. His head was hanging now, and tears dropped down onto the table, twinkling in the light. The Investigator stared at the droplets, suddenly wishing she were anywhere else than in that little room.

"Geoffrey," she said. "How do you think it happened?" She emphasized the you. "Please help me." Geoffrey sniffled. "I have to figure out why," she said. "And I think you can help. You're a very smart lad." Geoffrey dragged the back of his hand over his face, sniffing loudly again.

"Would you like a tissue?" asked Professor Zeke, quietly.

Geoffrey shook his head, but mumbled, "Can I go to the toilet?"

"Of course," said the Investigator. "Take your time."

Geoffrey stood up slowly and shuffled out of the room. The Principal and Arden, just outside, looked up expectantly as the door opened and the boy emerged. Zeke watched the door roll back shut. The Investigator dropped her head into her hands.

"Oh, I don't like this," she said.

"I think you're doing very well," Zeke said, a little awkwardly she felt. "For what it's worth." The Investigator snorted grimly. "Why," asked Zeke. "Did you go off script?"

The Investigator lifted her head, pulled the tablet to her, then slid it around on the table, bouncing it back and forth between her hands. She sighed. "He's been asked the same questions hundreds of times," she said. "And he always gives the same answers. And all the questions are asking if he did this thing or if he did that thing. If, if, if. And he always says no, no, no." She stopped playing with the tablet and looked up to the professor. "So I want to ask him how. Start by getting him to pretend it, and maybe there will be some truth in what he says."

Zeke nodded. "Have you," she hesitated, searching. "Worked with children before?" She hadn't wanted to say interrogated.

"No," the Investigator said. "Any tips?"

"Well." Zeke leaned back. "I can't give you any general tips, because each child here is like a whole different universe unto themselves. But for Geoffrey," she paused. What about Geoffrey. He was quieter than most of the other students, but certainly not the most reserved. He lost often at stones, because he played too aggressively. He loved the spy games the children played. His favorite authors came from eighth cycle Southern Hemisphere, but his writing most closely matched sub fifteen pre-dawn works in western Eurasia. He had broken his left arm more times than he could probably remember, but his right arm, his write arm, only once. Zeke shrugged. "Just remember that he's a real person."

The Investigator looked confused.

"He's not," Zeke sighed. "He's not a subject. He's not some experiment. Obviously he's not an adult, but he's not an alien. He's a person."

The Investigator nodded slowly. "Okay," she said.

Zeke laughed self-consciously. "I'm sorry," she said. "That didn't make much sense, did it?"

"I get you," said the Investigator.

The door opened and Geoffrey walked back in.

FIVE

THE TRAP

Professor bol Win sat on the edge of his bed, feet flat on the floor, hands on his knees, head forward, back as straight as it could be, and his eyes closed. His years pre-treatment had rounded his back a bit more than he liked. But he felt lucky all the same. No one here besides the Principal knew what it had felt like. They were all born into a world of privilege never before known in human history. How close he had been to missing it.

The debates at the time had focused on the ethics of it all. Completely arresting the aging process was developed for interstellar travel, so that humans could survive to see the planets they set out to find. And then it had spread to the families of the astronauts, because shouldn't they be allowed to see their loved ones again? And then it had spread a little further, and further still, all the while as people argued that it would create an unbearable strain on the planet's dwindling resources.

He remembered following the debate, being ever more aware of each day that passed, how he got one more day older. He couldn't disagree with the people who said that Earth couldn't withstand it. He couldn't disagree that the kind of population controls needed would be draconian, to say the least. He couldn't disagree with any of the arguments against providing the treatment to everyone. But he so desperately wanted it.

Eventually, there was no stopping it. People couldn't be turned away from the prospect of so much more life. Walking out of the health clinic that day had been remarkable. He still remembered. A feeling of relief so strong that he sat down on a stoop and cried. Crying like a newborn baby, which wasn't far from the truth. But newborn babies cry because they're upset, uncomfortable. He had been the opposite.

How long ago that was.

That city didn't even exist anymore. The planet had given a small sigh and shrugged it off one day. But no cities from that day existed anymore. Not really. Some might be in the same spots, and a few, remarkably, had the same names. But every scrap of material, every building, every brick, every thread had been replaced multiple times by now. Bol Win wondered if there was, in a city somewhere, a person who had never moved. Someone like him or the Principal - an original. And who had stayed in the same spot as the world changed and changed again. Maybe someone in Ayshata, who watched each time the Dante or the Virgil alighted back to Earth. Looked at the stars, but had never been. Could travel anywhere in the world, or the solar system, or the galaxy if they really wanted. But chose to stay right where they were. Because they had found a piece of comfort that they never wanted to give up.

How marvelous that would be. How lucky that person would be. Bol Win's breath came heavier.

Not like him. Stuck in a corner of the world no one wanted. Stuck because if he was anywhere else, he would be driven mad by not knowing what was happening here. No other professor had been here since the beginning. None of them had the same dedication to the cause. The real cause. Not what it had devolved into.

The Central Authority Administration would offer him the Principalship at some point. They had before, once, long ago. Back then, he had thought the best place to be was directly teaching. That was before the mood had shifted. Now they were all concerned about the children. This was precisely the time the school needed a leader to get them back on the right track. And it is what the school had lacked now for who knows how long.

And now this ridiculous case of plagiarism. It threatened everything he had worked for. How had that little shit read Carmilla? But maybe he could use this. Use it to petition a change.

Someone knocked on the door, startling him.

A student, judging from how high up it sounded, unless a teacher had crouched down to knock. Bol Win rose smoothly and went to his desk. His room was sparser than the other teachers. Apart from the same style bed, desk, and chairs that they all shared, the only personal piece he had was a tall bookcase.

The knock sounded like Greta.

"Please come in," bol Win said, sitting down at his desk, his back to the window.

Greta came into the room. Greta was an exceptional talent at twelfth and thirteenth era literature, both in analysis and mimicry. Her original work could easily be passed off as another writer. Belted, or even Salu. Bol Win hoped she could find a modern voice, however. At the moment, she looked downcast. Bol Win gestured to a chair.

Greta walked over and sat, leaving the door open. Her shoulders were hunched and her head was hanging. She lay her hands in her lap.

"My dear child," said bol Win. "What's the matter?"

She sniffed once. "Professor," Greta said, mournfully. "What will happen to Geoffrey?"

Bol Win blinked and leaned back in his chair. "I'm not sure," he said. "But he'll be treated fairly." Would he? Who knew, really?

"He didn't do anything wrong!" Greta said.

Bol Win blinked and leaned forward in his chair. "My child," he said softly, folding his hands together on his desk. "The young lad plagiarized."

"But."

"No," bol Win said, firmly. He sighed and turned his head. "We don't teach the mission much anymore, do we?" he said, aloud but to himself.

"I know the mission," said Greta.

"Do you?" he turned back to her. "And you know how plagiarism jeopardizes that mission?" He waited.

"Yes, professor," Greta said.

"And you know how important the mission is?"

"Yes, professor."

"Humanity is..." bol Win placed his hands flat on his desk. "Perishing. We need, all of us, need a renaissance. An outpouring of brilliance and creativity in the arts to spark the fires of our being. You, and the very special children like you in other schools, will be that spark." He ran a hand through his thinning hair. He felt panicky. "Greta," he said. The girl looked up. Her eyes were wide. "You don't know what it's like out there," bol Win said. "Not really. It's not something you can truly experience just by reading about it. You can't understand how deeply lost we have become."

"We?" Greta asked.

"Everyone," bol Win said. "All of humanity. As we have achieved so much technologically, we have lost our way. We have upset a balance." He paused. "We needed to do that, Greta." She nodded. "We needed to survive. But as we..." he stopped and closed his eyes. "When I was your age, we hadn't traveled to the stars." Greta stared at him. "And we lived in just the briefest glimpses of time. A flash and it was all behind you." Bol Win opened his eyes. "And now?" he said. "Now we live in a perpetual twilight," he said, quietly. "If we aren't careful, it will be the end of time."

The two, professor and student, sat in silence.

"But we've been here such a long time," Greta said finally. "When will we fix things?"

Part of the phrase caught in his mind and set it tumbling. "Such a long time," bol Win whispered.

"When will we fix things?" Greta repeated.

Bol Win seemed to bring himself back from a distant place. "Well, my child," he said. "Patience and time are what we do have. When you are ready, you will all be the most wonderful forces for good." Greta smiled. "But," bol Win continued. "It will be your imaginations that make that spark. And plagiarism is the antithesis of that goal. Not only is it the absence of imagination, it is the spirit of unearned greed and vanity that led to how we lost our way. It must not happen again," bol Win said.

Greta nodded solemnly. "But," she said. "It's not Geoffrey's fault."

Bol Win spread his hands. "I'm afraid it is," he said. "He copied that book."

"He couldn't have done it by himself!" Greta said. She looked directly at Professor bol Win. "He hasn't touched the library copy, so he must have seen another one. Someone here must have a secret library. How else could he have done it?"

"Oh," said bol Win. "Now. That's quite a thing to say. Who's been saying that?"

"No one," said Greta. "But how else?" she asked again.

"How else?" said bol Win, staring dumbly at her. "How else," he said. His gaze fell away slowly, down and to the left. His hand came to his face and he bit down on the end of his thumb. Greta watched him closely. Professor bol Win shook himself, then stood, then sat back down. "Now Greta," he said. "I don't want you talking about such nonsense. Go to your readings."

"Yes, professor," Greta said quietly. She got up and walked out, looked back at the professor as she closed the door. He had turned and was staring out the window.

He heard the door close behind him as light washed down over his face. "Such a long time," he breathed.

The Principal and Arden walked side by side on the path around the school. There were clues that soon the heat would become more oppressive. An oven blast wind now and again came skittering over the dust and pebbles, ruffling their habits. The Principal's thoughts wandered with the wind.

There was a time when this walk would have been fatal. The radiation would simply have cooked them alive. And yet now here they were. Even further back they would have been trudging through ice and snow, regardless of the season. Can you imagine? Further still and what then? What was this land like, connected to all the other land masses? A giant supercontinent, split apart. But wouldn't all the pieces crash into each other again? The Principal frowned, trying to remember his plate tectonics.

Could he see such a thing? It was a ridiculous notion. Even with this perpetual longevity they were still barely a blink in the geologic record. Weren't they? What was a blink anyway? And how long had they even been here anyway? What a peculiar existence they had managed to craft for themselves. As if they had slipped the clutches of time. It had lost so much meaning the instant its grasp had loosened on their consciousness. Now here he was, walking a path that hadn't existed in his lifetime and could very well fall out of existence in his lifetime. Paved over maybe, or obliterated by tides or rocks. Or simply become overtaken by dust and fade away. Maybe a meteor would strike this very spot when somehow all the humans had gone.

But in this moment, right now, he felt as if he had been

walking on this path forever and would never be able to stop.

"I always wished I had Monsieur Dupin's skills at mentalism," Arden said.

The Principal laughed. "Trying to read my thoughts?"

"Trying. You seemed quite deep in them. The investigation?"

The Principal chuckled again. "Tidal waves and radiation, if you must know," he said. "Although I would guess your thoughts are bent toward the case at hand, particularly if the world's first detective is on your mind." Arden murmured assent. "And how do you suppose our own Dupin is managing?" asked the Principal.

Arden shrugged as another rush of wind pushed past them. "Fine, I suppose. Not what I expected."

"No, indeed. Me neither." The Principal smiled to himself. He glanced at his walking companion. "You're not terribly pleased they're here." It wasn't unkind but it also wasn't a question.

"No," said Arden. The Principal saw the man's teeth clench then relax. "I suppose it's silly," he said, finally.

"What is?"

Arden gave an embarrassed laugh. "I can't help but think," he stopped, frustrated. "I just don't trust them," he blurted out.

"Don't trust them?"

"No," said Arden. "I can't shake the feeling that they're going to try and weaponize what we're doing somehow."

"Weaponize?" The Principal was surprised. He was aware he was stupidly repeating what Arden was saying, but he couldn't help himself.

"I know it's ridiculous," Arden muttered.

"How would they weaponize children?" asked the Principal.

"I don't know," Arden said, still annoyed. "You don't follow the genetic development updates. If they could control the aging process more, they could condition children for longer before aging them up."

"If they could do that," said the Principal. "They could age these children up. That would be wonderful."

Arden grunted. "Maybe." He stared straight ahead.

"Besides," said the Principal. "Why would they need to do that? Condition them like that?"

"Stronger officers," said Arden. "Maybe give them more control of the development of their conscience, or maybe keep it from developing at all."

"They're not still developing officers, are they?"

"I don't think that Officer Third is terribly old," said Arden.

The Principal waved his hands dismissively. "I don't think we need to worry about that right now," he said. "The main thing is that our children are being taken care of." Arden grunted in agreement. The two continued in silence for a moment.

"Something else," said Arden. The Principal turned his head slightly in acknowledgment. "Apparently," Arden paused, wondering how to word it. "All the children visited their mentors."

"What?" the Principal was taken aback.

"All at different times over the course of the day."

The Principal creased his forehead. "What for?"

Arden shrugged but the Principal missed the gesture. "They were all asking about Geoffrey. What would happen to him."

"Did Geoffrey meet with Zeke?"

"No."

"Did they ask anything else?"

"That was all the faculty told me about."

The Principal turned to stare at Arden with a bewildered face. "What are they after?"

Arden shrugged again, visibly to the Principal this time. "Not sure. Usually they're better with their spy craft." The Principal snorted. "A bit heavy-handed this time."

"They never expect us to actually talk to each other," the Principal said. He continued walking in silence for a few moments.

"Should we let Monsieur Dupin know?" asked Arden.

The Principal threw his hands up. "Just kids being kids."

"Just kids being kids?!"

"That's what..." Lin stopped and thought. "Arden said the Principal said."

"That's ridiculous." Zeke flopped backward onto her bed.

Lin sat in her visiting chair in the corner idly running his thumbnail along the wall. He should be writing. Classes postponed. It was the perfect time for it. So why was he so irritated? On edge with everything. "What do you think it is?" And that edge slipped into the question, even if it was unintended.

Zeke sat up again. "They're probing." She said it as if it was the most obvious thing on the world.

"Probing." Lin raised and lowered his eyebrows with his gaze still on his thumb.

"Yes," said Zeke. She stared intently at the ground. "They're probing," she repeated to herself. "They know something's not right and they're trying to get information."

Lin had stood in a house with plaster walls once. If you'd been running your fingers over the walls there, they were liable to flake off. Not here. Here the stone and plastic would last for who knew how long. He'd been running his thumbnail over this same patch for a long time. And never so much as a scratch. Was there anything anywhere that he'd made a mark on?

"Are you listening to me?"

"What?"

"They're trying-"

"They're not," Lin started. "What information?"

"I don't know!" Zeke was exasperated. "But look at it. They ask the same question to everybody and they look for something off. It's the same thing the Investigator would do on a case."

"So what." Something started to build up inside of him.

"So they're investigating something!"

"An investigation. They're just kids." It felt like panic but what was he panicking about?

"You know perfectly well that's not true. What's the matter with you?"

Suddenly he was up and out of the chair, pacing rapidly in the small room. His hands were gripped tight to one another. His face was contorted.

"Hey," Zeke said softly. "What's wrong, Lin?"

His breath was shallow and rapid.

"Come sit next to me."

The room was so small and impenetrable. Walls that would stop an army. There was the door and where would it go? The whole school was a suffocating prison. He could make it outside and be in a wasteland. The sky crushing down on him.

"Come sit next to me."

Her voice came through. With a ragged sigh he sat down on the bed. Her arm came around him, pulling him close, and his head dropped to her shoulder. She felt his chest rise, inhaling deeply.

"It's okay," she said.

They sat in silence.

"Do you know," Zeke said after a time. "When I first came here, one of the first things I noticed, and absolutely loved, was the silence. It's so peaceful. Before where I lived, there was always some background noise. Traffic or technology or just people. I remember my first night here, laying on this bed, and just reveling at the peace."

After a moment, Lin spoke. "Could you sleep?"

Zeke laughed. "No."

"Me neither."

She squeezed him tighter and he pressed his forehead to her shoulder. "You okay?"

He nodded. "Yeah," he said quietly. "I just feel so strange. I don't know what it is. It feels like..." Zeke waited. "It feels like I've been here forever," he said. "And I'll never leave."

"Don't be silly."

He stared blankly at the wall, feeling the warmth of her arm. "I am all in a sea of wonders," he said, softly. "I doubt; I fear; I think strange things."

Zeke smiled. "Which you dare not confess?"

"Even to my own soul," Lin said. Zeke laughed. "The Investigator will sort it all out," Lin said, after a moment.

"Hmm," Zeke frowned. "I wish I had your confidence." She absentmindedly rubbed his shoulder. "What's with those officers? Why are they even here?"

"Oh, they're alright." His voice stayed flat and quiet.

"What's that line on the arm of one?" Lin didn't respond. "Have you seen it? It's like a..." she shook her head. "I don't even know what. An armlet? It's a perfectly-"

"It's a scar," Lin said.

"What? No, that's not it. It's a perfectly straight line around his arm. It's just below the elbow." She felt his head nod slowly on her shoulder.

"It's a scar."

Zeke looked down at the top of Lin's head. "How is that possible?"

He was quiet for a few moments, then spoke. "We..." Lin stopped, checking himself. "Soldiers have regenerative tissue stored permanently. In the event of a catastrophic injury, the tissue is used to regrow missing parts. Then the new piece is fused on."

"Fused?"

He shrugged. "That's what we called it." He gave a small laugh. "A big shiny laser that zapped everything together. Lose an arm? Grow a new one and paste it on. But it leaves that scar."

"That's awful," Zeke shuddered.

"Mm," Lin murmured. "Cheaper than a new soldier."

Zeke shook her head. "Do you have any scars?" she asked quietly.

Lin nodded.

She waited.

"Do you think we'll ever leave this place?" he asked.

Zeke reached and put her other arm around him. "I know we will," she said.

The Investigator bolted upright in her bed. The tint on the windows kept the room dark. She heard someone stir across the room.

"Chief?" Brighton asked, hazily.

"How long have we been here?" the Investigator asked. Tyrick and Third were both snoring softly.

"It's, uh," Brighton was still half asleep, she could tell. He probably wouldn't even remember this. "It's been a few," he paused. "I can pull up the log."

"No," the Investigator said. "Go back to sleep."

With a murmur, he was gone.

Her dream still pressed down on her. It had been black. Nothing. Not even the void of space could compare. An infinite nothingness where her consciousness hung suspended. She knew beyond a shadow of a doubt that she was dead, that this was the afterlife. And it terrified her. An entire eternity of blank space.

Now she was awake, she felt two things. One, an immense relief that she was, in fact, awake. That it had just been a dream. A bed and walls around her. And two, the lingering dread that it wasn't just a dream at all.

"You should have seen him," said Greta. "He looked like the kind of person who thinks they're being clever, but everyone and their cousin can see they're hiding something."

The children, minus Geoffrey, were in a classroom. Writing desks were neatly laid out in rows, but the occupants were almost all clustered in a lump near the back of the room. Shinty sat by the door, keeping an eye out.

They were supposed to be scattered around the building, working on free writing. But that's all they'd been doing since classes stopped. Pency just wanted to get back to normal. To sit in class like they always did.

Max nodded. "Okay," he said. "Anyone else notice something strange?"

Heads shook. Greta looked around with determination. "It's Professor bol Win."

Pency stared at the floor. He wanted most of all to go and talk to his friend. How must he have been doing with all of this? Keeping this secret? Not talking to anyone but the teachers? Pency felt ashamed. He had gone along with the silent treatment.

"We need to flush him out," Stephen was saying. "Stress him, follow him, and find the books."

"How many do you think he has?"

"There's no telling. He's probably been adding to his collection since he got here."

He had thought it was the right thing to do at the time. He'd let himself be convinced by Stephen. That it would really help Geoffrey. Make him tell the truth somehow. But it had just caused him more pain.

"We'll have to set up a rotation to follow him," Lulu said.

"That's a good idea," Max agreed. "He's got to go to it sometime."

"But we still need to scare him," said Stephen. "I'll take care of that."

"We'll need interference."

"And cover stories."

"Sort the rotation based on a double chore plan."

"What are we going to do about nights?"

"That's probably the most likely time. We have to be watching every minute."

"Hey!"

Everyone turned to stare at Pency. Even Shinty looked back.

"We need to talk to Geoffrey," Pency said. The room fell silent and still. The shame that had built up in Pency now began to creep out and spread across the other students. Stephen looked grim.

"We can't risk it."

"Risk what?" Pency said. "It's the only way to get confirmation."

"We can get our own confirmation," said Stephen. "And what if we talk to him, and then he turns around and spills everything to Professor bol Win?"

"He's not going to do that."

"How do you know? If he's covering for him, they might be in on it together. For all we know-"

"Shut up!" Pency shouted. Stephen blinked. "Shut! Up! Something fucked up is going on, and we are going to fix it, because no one else will. Someone is messing with Geoffrey. He wouldn't be doing this without a reason. Either he's being tricked into this, or," Pency struggled to find the word.

"Coerced?" offered Lulu.

"Yes!" Pency said, still angry. "Or coerced. Or there's something even more fucked up going on. Either way, it is not his fault. It's the fault of whoever or whatever is doing this to him. And we are not going to punish him for that." Pency stopped and glared at the other students. Max and Lulu were nodding slowly. Wint looked sad. Greta had a determined set to her jaw. Even Stephen looked chastened. "I'm going to talk to him," Pency said.

He stood up and walked out of the room, and the rest of the children followed.

Geoffrey sat on his bunk, mindlessly dragging a pen in looping circles in his journal. He hadn't written anything in quite a while. Not since he'd first been brought to the Principal's office. It was difficult to get the words to come. And when they did, when he thought of a phrase or an idea for a story, he could never be sure if it was really his.

What if it happened again? What if he wrote something and got escorted back to the Principal's office. What if he had to make that same walk again, walking next to Professor Arden, the feeling of fear heavy in the air. And once he got into the room, it would only get worse. They'd never believe him. Not if it happened again. He'd be expelled for sure. Any story could be his last.

So he doodled. Probably copying some great abstract painter. They could kick him out for that.

He heard the other students come in and glanced up, then did a double-take. They were looking at him. And walking toward him. Pency was right at the front. Were they going to kill him off?

The Investigator walked slowly down the hall of the vacant faculty quarters, playing back in her mind her conversation with Professor Zeke.

"You're Geoffrey's adviser?"

"That's right."

"How's he doing through all this?"

The teacher had been helpful, non-evasive. She hadn't displayed any signs of deception. There had also been real concern for her student. A kindness and a warmth, even though it seemed she was wary of her interrogator at first. The Investigator had interviewed her last of all the faculty. Now she walked past the rooms of all those she had spoken to. Peering in, it all struck her as so monastic. They really lived like this? The rooms were all so sparse. And similar. Yet here and there were little deviations. Symbols of the personalities maybe.

If the boy had received help, maybe there would be a clue here. A symbol of resistance. Or maybe she was just grasping at straws.

"I'm not sure. I think he's having trouble with the other students."

"Trouble?"

"Shutting him out. You know, their own kind of punishment."

She stopped at Professor Zeke's room. There was an extra chair and a small table with a chess board set up. Probably for Lin. Most often, anyway. They seemed to be on intimate terms. She frowned. A rug with an intricate geometric pattern. A necklace hanging above a desk. And strands of slow-ivy, three of them, crawling up the walls and spreading across the ceiling. They must have been growing for centuries.

The Investigator continued walking.

"What do you think his punishment should be?"

She had sighed. The Investigator couldn't remember seeing anyone with such a helpless expression. The professor's whole body had just crumpled inside. The

Investigator moved on.

"We're looking into the possibility that he was assisted by a member of the faculty."

"Assisted?"

The deception analysis could be done afterward, but she had known at the time what it would show. The surprise was genuine. "Can you think of anyone who might have been involved?" They couldn't help but think of a name. It was just human nature. "Someone came to mind just now. Who was it?"

"No," she had said. She had been the only one to refuse. "When you leave, we'll still be here. We'll have to live with whatever fallout you create. I'll not turn on my colleagues based on my own biased feelings."

It was a good answer. A very respectable one. It made the Investigator feel slightly guilty for having asked everyone the same question already. They had all said the same name. She stopped at his room. It was sparser than the others. Few symbols. Few places to keep secrets.

The children had all done interviews of the professors. They were conducting their own investigation, the little imps. Which kid had it been who'd talked to this one? The tallish girl, the inquisitive one. Maybe she had stirred something up.

SIX

THE NOTE

Wind crackled across the sea, spitting water and foam into the air, before sweeping up the stony beach. Tiny dust tornados spun into shape before dissipating over the rocks. The landscape, usually so quiet and still, emitted a low whistle now, like a warning. If there had been birds or beasts, they would have taken to nest or scuttled under a rock. But there was nothing here. Only the wind and the school and its inhabitants, both permanent and visiting.

Now the wind came crawling toward the low building, at great speed, before breaking on the stone walls. The air currents split apart violently, but pushed on, tumbling around corners and over the roof, howling through the courtyard.

In the late dusk, the sun had already crept out of sight, and the sky was darkening quickly. Inside, the occupants of the school were in their rooms or dormitory. Classrooms sat dim and empty, unused formally now for some time. Chores had been completed, and stew for the following day was slowly cooking in the kitchen.

A single person was out of place.

Geoffrey lay flat on his stomach, the top of his head peering out around a corner, looking down the corridor of the faculty living quarters, watching it grow darker. Lulu and Greta had been against the idea of him going. Why not someone else? If he were caught, with everything else on his record, he'd certainly be expelled. Another student might simply get extra chores.

But Geoffrey was adamant. He didn't know anything about a secret book. He didn't know anything about getting help from a professor. Whatever was going on was being done to him, and he wanted to know who was pulling the strings. So he waited, watching to see if their prime suspect would take the bait. The hall lights had been turned out, and the last of the sun faded, leaving nothing but inky darkness. Geoffrey felt terrified. He waited, unaware of the conversation taking place back in the student quarters.

"This is stupid," Stephen said. "If they are working together, we'll get nothing. Or worse. Some kind of misdirection."

Pency was trying to ignore him.

"We didn't give him a chance before," said Greta. "We should give him a chance now."

Stephen scoffed and continued pacing, but was silent. The waiting was unbearable.

"Will you sit down?" Shinty said. All the other students were in their bunks.

Geoffrey strained his ears. Was that movement behind a door? Several still had lights on, but the dull glow wouldn't cast a shadow. Or would it? A door opened. Geoffrey's heart leapt into his throat.

Professor Nalin emerged with a sigh and headed down the hall, away from Geoffrey, toward the washroom.

"Lay down!" Lulu snapped.

"Someone should be a backup," Stephen said, still pacing.

Max groaned. "We went over this. Two out is more risky. It's more chance they get caught out there, and it's more chance it gets noticed in here if there's a night check."

"There hasn't been a night check in orbits."

"That's not even true. You just sleep through them."

Stephen violently sat down on his bunk. "It's too risky not to," he said. "We need to make sure he's not double-crossing, and even if he isn't," he quickly added as Greta glared at him. "If he gets caught or in trouble, we need to know."

The children were silent.

"I'll go," Pency said.

"You might protect him if he's crossing," said Stephen. "Besides!" he said loudly, over Pency's curses. "Your beds are too close. They'd notice in a check." Pency gritted his teeth. "I'll go," said Stephen.

"You've been trying to trip him up since the beginning of this mess!" Pency snapped.

"So what?"

"So you'd probably let him get caught!"

"I'll go!" Greta shouted. "Either of you two idiots would make enough noise to bring down a banshee." She slid off her bunk and was out the door.

The door closest to Geoffrey opened and light spilled across the hallway again. Geoffrey's whole body contracted, and he barely managed to contain a yelp. Entirely unaware of the petrified child laying on the floor just meters away, Professor Arden stepped out and headed toward the washroom. Poor Geoffrey's hands were clenched tight, and he could feel perspiration trickle down his sides. He inched backward until his head was clear, then rested it on the cold floor.

This had clearly been a mistake. One of the other students could do this. That would be for the best.

He heard Professor Nalin and Professor Arden conversing quietly. Taking a deep breath, he nosed out into the hall, straining his ears.

"A better eye," said Professor Nalin, who was facing his direction. Professor Arden nodded and said something. "Are you sure?" asked Professor Nalin. Professor Arden made some affirmatory noises, and Professor Nalin nodded. "Well, good night then." And went into his room. Professor Arden continued to the washroom.

Geoffrey let out a sigh. As the washroom door closed, he

heard a click behind him. He startled again, but recovered faster at the familiar sound. Looking back, he couldn't make anything out in the corridor, let alone who was there. He started to crawl backward, his habit bunching at his knees. Slowly getting to his feet, he risked a little noise, clicking his tongue once in reply. A three note click followed. Greta. The two children gradually made their way to each other in the dark.

Signing was impossible. Geoffrey put his head to Greta's ear and breathed. "What are you doing here?"

"Keep an extra eye out," she breathed back into his ear.

"Local light ten percent," Professor Arden said, rounding the corner. A dull illumination appeared over his head on the ceiling, following him.

The children melted backward. Geoffrey into a classroom, and Greta down the hall to the kitchen. Geoffrey was in the faculty conference room. The door was always open, unless a meeting was going on. He ducked behind the door and flattened out on the ground again, peering through the gap between the door and the frame. Geoffrey held his breath.

Professor Arden quietly walked past, the small circle of light following him. The sandals made almost no noise, and the light barely registered, and there was quickly no trace of the professor. Geoffrey wished it wasn't so dark. He wished he were asleep in his bunk. He wished that his story had been his own, and that none of this had happened.

He heard Greta's footsteps and barely saw her outline slipping into the room. "Where are you?" she hissed. Geoffrey shuffled back from behind the door. "He's doing a bed check!" she hissed again.

"I know."

"We're going to get caught!"

"There's nothing we can do about it," Geoffrey whispered.

Inside, he had felt sick to his stomach, but only for just a moment. The fear had risen, the terror of being found out and kicked out of school. And then it had vanished. It didn't matter now. All he could do was try to trap Professor bol Win, and maybe find out how he had tricked Geoffrey into copying that book. He didn't care about anything else.

"Geoffrey!" Greta shook his arm.

He looked at her in the dark and grinned. "Who cares?" he whispered. "Come on. We can't wait in the hallway in case Professor Arden comes back. We'll have to wait here. I've got a good spot behind the door." He led her back to his hiding place, and the two crouched down.

"What did the note say anyway?" Greta whispered.

Panic gripped Geoffrey yet again. The note. He had forgotten the note. Slowly, he reached into his right habit sleeve, into the pocket. He felt the folded up paper and drew it out.

"You didn't deliver the note!" Greta was incredulous. Geoffrey shut his eyes. "Do you know how much trouble we could get in right now? And he's not even going to budge!"

"We," Geoffrey swallowed, his throat dry. "We can try again tomorrow."

"If Professor Arden sees the empty beds, then we're out of it."

All of his confidence from a moment ago had deserted him. He was going in a hundred different directions. And now what? What were the odds of a bed check tonight? What if this was the last chance he would be given? Time, the one thing they had ever in abundance, had abandoned them. So now he could sit back and hope they wouldn't get caught and he wouldn't get expelled before they could find the answer to this riddle, or he could keep fighting.

Professor Arden quietly opened the door to the student quarters. The light above him diffused across the room, darkening as it did so, keeping the room still very dim, but light enough to make out sleeping forms in beds. The professor scanned across the room. His eyes came to rest on Geoffrey's bunk. The boy was curled into a tight ball, facing away, sleeping soundly. An enviable quality, really. Professor Arden wished he could get to sleep like that. Since this had all begun, it was getting more and more difficult. And yet there the boy was. The cause of all of it. Fast asleep.

Professor Arden gritted his teeth and turned away, walking out of the room, taking care to close the door silently behind him. Had he looked closer to his left as he was leaving, he might have noticed Greta's empty bunk. As the light extinguished in the room, Pency turned over in Geoffrey's bunk.

"I've got to drop it off now," Geoffrey said. He started shuffling backward again, a part of him hoping that Greta would stop him. Have a better idea somehow.

"Hurry!" she whispered.

He sighed and crept to the doorway.

"Wait!" Greta darted out. "If you get caught, you're expelled. Give it to me." She reached for the note. Geoffrey pulled back. "Don't be stupid. We don't have time." She snatched it and slipped out of the room. Geoffrey stood there, blinking.

Greta walked on tiptoes down the hall, keeping her hand on the stone wall. She found the corner and peeked down the teacher's quarters. Professor Arden's door was shut, but the light in his room was still on. It crept out from under the door, providing the barest of help, but it was enough. Professor bol Win's room was the next one down.

Hardly daring to breathe, she moved down the hall to her target. His light was out. Even if she slid the note under his door, he wouldn't find it until the morning. In the morning they might all be in detention.

She slipped the folded piece of paper under the door, then ran her fingernails along the length of the bottom of the door. Turning, she darted back up the hallway. Around the corner, and there was Professor Arden, halfway down the hall already. Greta ducked back and flattened against the wall. She was trapped.

To her left, the light in Professor bol Win's room came on. Greta saw the illumination peek out from under the door. In a moment, he would open it to see who was there. Without thinking, Greta sped down the corridor, past Professor bol Win's room, toward the washroom. She had almost reached it when she heard the door open behind her.

Instinctively, Greta collapsed into the corner of the end of the hall. The washroom door was right in front of her, but she couldn't risk the noise, or the movement. All she could do was hope she was deep enough in the shadows. Without breathing, she slowly turned her head to look back. And there he was. Looking right at her.

Professor bol Win looked back and forth, seeing nothing but a dark hallway. And a light from under Professor Arden's door. He stepped back into his room and closed the door.

Greta inched toward the washroom door, and froze again as Professor Arden walked into view. He briskly stepped into his own room, and the light extinguished from under his door. He must not have noticed the empty beds.

Now what? Greta considered making her way back to Geoffrey, but Professor bol Win's light was still on. She would have to hide in the washroom and hope no one needed to use the facilities. Until his light was out, she couldn't risk him leaving his room right as she was walking past. Carefully, she eased her way into the washroom, keeping the door ajar. She wondered how Geoffrey was doing at the other end of the hallway, probably still crouched in the conference room. Not knowing where she was or if she'd managed to deliver the note.

Suddenly, the light in Professor bol Win's room went out. He wasn't biting. She let out a deep breath. All she had to do now was get back across the hallway, and they could get back to their bunks. And try again tomorrow.

The hallway was pitch black now. She couldn't see her hand in front of her face. Greta gently walked out, keeping her hand on the wall again. Just slow and steady, and don't trip. Don't make any noise. Don't sneeze. She began to make her way down the hall.

A door opened. She couldn't see it, but she heard it. And she knew who it was. Professor bol Win had been here since the school started. He didn't need light to get around. She heard the door close, and heard the soft sound of sandals making their way down the hall. Greta stood frozen, a statue affixed to the wall.

Was he gone? He had to be. What if he had stopped? What if he was checking his tracks? What if his secret hiding place was in the conference room and he'd found Geoffrey and melted his brain with his radio-wave device? Greta closed her eyes, and willed herself to move forward. Step by step she made her way back. She knew there was a window across from the door of each faculty room, and she counted them off as she passed. When she reached the last one, she allowed herself a little more speed, and quickened her pace.

The wall abruptly vanished as she reached the corner, just a bit sooner than she had expected. She floundered for a moment in the dark, not having something solid to stay grounded with. But she recovered and continued on, feeling her way in the dark for the conference room door. She finally made it and stepped inside.

"Geoffrey," she whispered. There was nothing. Looking behind the door, she knew he had gone. After Professor bol Win in the dark.

Geoffrey felt nothing as he shadowed Professor bol Win through the school. Not fear, or doubt, or anger. Not glee or excitement. His mind was blank; only instinctively processing his movement and that of his quarry. How to be as quiet as possible while keeping the professor in close enough proximity so that he didn't lose him in the night. Professor bol Win had been here since the school opened. But so had Geoffrey.

They made their way past classrooms and closets. For a moment, Geoffrey thought they were headed toward the library, but they continued past the stairwell for it. They continued on, until Professor bol Win opened an outer door and stepped out into the courtyard, closing the door behind him. Geoffrey cursed inside. He couldn't open the door until Professor bol Win was out of earshot. And he wouldn't know when that was. And even if he did, by the time he got outside, he'd never be able to see the professor.

But the wind had been sharp. Geoffrey had heard it when Professor bol Win had opened the door. Maybe it would cover the noise just enough. Before he could reconsider, Geoffrey turned the handle and was outside.

Starlight was the only help now. The wind came in gusts, tugging at his habit, shuddering through the courtyard. The occasional howl made Geoffrey duck. And there was Professor bol Win, rapidly fading into the dark. Geoffrey stepped quickly after him. There was more danger now. If Professor bol Win turned around, he would see the boy following him. Geoffrey strayed to the wall, hoping he would be less visible than in the open.

The professor did not turn though, and was soon on the grounds, walking along the path that circled the school. Geoffrey stepped from the courtyard, and his foot caught a rock. He fell forward, his hands reaching out and catching himself on the gravel pathway. He heard the small pebbles scrape together under his hands. The noise was unbearable.

There was no way to know if Professor bol Win had heard. Geoffrey kept his head down, staring at the stony ground, hoping that no challenge would be issued. If the professor noticed the noise enough to turn around, there was no indication. There was no shout. No angry steps back to the boy on his hands and knees in the rocks.

Geoffrey couldn't follow. He could fall too easily. His feet would make too much noise on the gravel. There was no way to continue. Professor bol Win had gotten away.

SEVEN

THE PLAN

Professor Zeke knocked on the Principal's office door before opening it and stepping inside. The Principal was at his desk and looked up.

"Good morning," Zeke said. "You wanted to see me?"

The Principal stood. "Yes, indeed. Let's go for a walk. It's too stuffy in here."

"The wind's picked up outside," Zeke said.

"Excellent," the Principal smiled and led Zeke out. He didn't speak while they made their way through the school. Zeke let him lead, patient and slightly confused. She had worried about the Principal since this whole incident began. The stress of the case had clearly taken a toll. But whenever she felt like it had gotten to be too much for him, he bounced right back and was his old self the next day. She wondered what kind of day this was.

The Principal walked contentedly through the halls. He looked forward to the wind each year. Howls and shrieks and shuddering doors if you left them open. The landscape was usually so lifeless but the wind gave it movement and a personality.

They wound their way up a staircase and emerged onto the roof. A rushing sound enveloped them, whipping their habits and hair. The Principal smiled and strode across the gravel with Zeke following. He stopped at the edge, resting his hands on the short wall, staring out across the rocks. Zeke joined him, closing her eyes and letting the wind press against her.

"Isn't it beautiful?" the Principal shouted.

Zeke opened her eyes, taking in the barren view. It was strange to think of it as beautiful. She had looked at these rocks for millennia. Could something so familiar still be beautiful in her eyes? She thought of Lin's face and knew the answer. Turning to the Principal, Zeke smiled and nodded.

"It's like..." the Principal shouted. "Like a poem. The wind and the rocks." He stared out, squinting against the air rushing against his eyes. "It's beautiful," he said, too softly for Zeke to hear.

"Are you..." Zeke started but stopped. She was going to ask if he was feeling well. But of course he was. He was acting strangely but what would asking him get? Just a routine exchange. He had wanted to meet for a reason and he would say what it was.

The Principal turned halfway to her, expectantly. When the second half of the question didn't come, he smiled and nodded to her. "Do you know how long this school has been here?" he shouted. Zeke shook her head. She had often wondered. "Too long. We've been here too long." He turned back to look over the desert.

"I don't follow," Zeke shouted.

The Principal nodded again. "This school," he shouted. He turned to her. "This school was meant to usher in a new renaissance of creativity for humanity. But all we've done is sit here, day after day, year after year, cycle after cycle."

"But," Zeke felt awkward. "That was only ever a pipe dream." Saying it out loud wasn't done. It was just what they accepted.

"Yes," the Principal shouted. "But we're going to try all the same." Zeke's eyes opened wide in surprise. The Principal laughed. "The problem that led to this school is still there. These children should never have been..." he paused, searching. "Sacrificed," he shouted. "They were sacrificed to try and cure the ills we brought upon ourselves. It was wrong.

But we have a chance to try and build something out of it. All we've done is care for them."

"That's a noble cause," Zeke shouted. "To care for them."

The Principal bobbed up and down in agreement. "It is," he shouted. "But it's not enough. We owe it to them to make their sacrifice worthwhile."

A blast of wind hit them hard and Zeke stepped backward. She was struggling. "What?" she shouted. "How?" Questions were swirling around her. "Why now?"

The Principal laughed uproariously and held his arms open against the wind. "Why not?" His habit caught the air currents and billowed out. "Isn't it glorious?" he shouted.

The Investigator sat on a rock. The wind had finally calmed a bit, and it was even a bit pleasant outside now. And just being under the sun and the sky was a luxury. Their room was spacious enough and the school was more than accommodating but she had spent most of her life in space, trapped inside a small can hurtling through stars. To stare out at a horizon was marvelous.

Tyrick, Brighton, and Third sat close by. Even Third kept quiet as the four enjoyed the breeze and the view. Finally, she had to break it.

"Anything to report?"

"No, chief."

"No, chief."

"Nope."

The Investigator surveyed the land, thinking about what might have been built here at some point if conditions were just slightly different. She withdrew her tablet and thought it on. The report readout flashed through. "Here's what we know so far." The three officers glanced over. She stared at the screen. The three officers waited patiently. "You already know what we know so far," the Investigator said. Now the three officers exchanged glances with one another.

But they did already know. The Principal must have been rubbing off on her. What was the point of going over the very same information that they already knew? Except as some pointless exercise in time wasting.

The Investigator looked up at them. "I have no clue how the boy copied that book." She waited a moment. "Ideas?"

"Well," said Tyrick. "What about the notion that he was helped?"

The Investigator shook her head. "We need some new ideas. Nothing is too far out there."

"Nothing?" asked Third. The Investigator nodded.

"Do these need to be verifiable?" asked Tyrick.

"What about mind control?" asked Third.

"No," the Investigator said to Tyrick. "What else?" she said to Third.

"What if he memorized it ages ago and has been waiting for a time when he thought no one would notice it?" asked Brighton.

"Okay," said the Investigator. "Seems unlikely, given that it was a perfect replica, and that he should have known it would get noticed. But that's a second option now."

The three officers sat.

"Chance?" asked Tyrick.

The Investigator shrugged. "It's technically a possibility but the odds of it are incalculably small. And considering we know all the variables and still couldn't properly compute a number, that's pretty small. There's a greater likelihood that the universe will collapse in this instant."

Third looked around. "We're still here."

"Oh, maybe we're not," said Brighton. "What if this is a simulation?"

"What is?" asked Third.

"All of it."

"Are we all in on it?"

"Maybe just I am," said Brighton.

"That's my luck," said Third. "Not only am I stuck here, I'm not actually even here."

"No, you're back home somewhere and I'm plugged into a machine."

"That might be good."

"What else?" said the Investigator.

"Time travel?" asked Tyrick. Third laughed. "Nothing off the table," said Tyrick. "He memorized it then went back in time to write it."

"You can't go back in time," said Brighton.

"Is nothing off the table just an expression?" asked Tyrick.

The Investigator let out an exasperated sigh. "We still don't have any kind of motive," she said. "No matter how he did it, we still don't know why it happened."

"It has to be sabotage," said Tyrick. The other three looked at him. "What does the act do? It discredits the school. This is supposed to be some bastion of creativity, right? So how does it look when one of their students is accused of plagiarism of all things. This is an attempt to derail their mission."

"Which mission though?" asked Brighton. "The original one or the current one?"

"Are those different?" asked Third. "What's the original one?"

"Do you pay any attention to case reports?" Brighton snapped. "They were supposed to..." he stalled, gesturing helplessly. "I don't know, save humanity or something. Spark a creative renaissance."

"Oh, right," said Third.

"If someone was trying to derail the original mission," the Investigator said. "It probably wasn't bol Win. He's a fanatic about it. But if they wanted to return..." she emphasized. "... to the original mission, they might want to derail the current mission."

"What's the current mission?" asked Third.

"Keep these kids relatively comfortable while we wait for the heat death of the universe," said Brighton sharply.

"That puts the focus back on bol Win," said Tyrick.

"It's a fuzzy plan," said Third. "How does plagiarism get them back to saving humanity? It makes more sense if they were trying to kill the creativity stuff."

"So who would want to do that?" asked Brighton.

"My money's on Professor Nalin," said Third.

"What? Why on the world would you say that?" asked Tyrick.

"It's always the person you least suspect."

"That has literally never been true in any of our cases," said the Investigator. "Any other motives?" she asked. The three were quiet again. "What if someone was trying to discredit the boy?"

"Discredit? Why would they want to do that?" asked Tyrick.

The Investigator shrugged. "A rival? Another student."

"Another student? How could they have pulled it off though?"

"I don't know," the Investigator frowned. "But other students had access to the book at some point. Not recently, but we know they were in contact with it. What if..." she trailed off, not knowing where to go.

"What if someone manipulated him into it? Subconsciously," said Third. "We've seen how they get into their spy craft and mind games. What if this was a new kind of game."

"That would be a nightmare of a thing to pull off," said Brighton. "Letter for letter?" Third shrugged. "Still though, there are some strange dynamics going on with these kids."

"What if his adviser wanted to get him kicked out for some reason?" asked Third.

"Zeke?" said Tyrick. "I like Zeke. Besides, she didn't show any flags on deception, right?" The Investigator nodded.

"No one threw any major flags," said Third. "Someone's doing an adept job at hiding something. And I don't trust the people who seem too good. It's always the person you least suspect."

"That's true," said the Investigator. "In every case we've ever had, that's how it's turned out."

"So we've narrowed it down to every single person in the school," said Brighton.

"That's progress," said Third. "When we started, I didn't think any of the other kids were involved. And now look. We've got even more suspects."

"Excuse me," Tyrick said. He looked apologetic. "Is this even necessary? It's not really our purpose here after all."

The Investigator gave a sharp look at her first officer. To his credit, he didn't wither. He had been the recipient of such looks from her many times before and, at least in this case, he had the advantage of being correct. Brighton and Third still kept their mouths shut.

"As far as you are concerned, we have two objectives here," the Investigator said, curtly.

"Should we be doing anything about the first one?" Tyrick asked, testing the limits of the Investigator's patience.

"I expect if you should be doing something, I would have told you about it. Yes?" The Investigator arched an eyebrow. Tyrick put his head down.

"Someone's coming," said Third.

The four waited, casually looking back out at the sea, enjoying the wind. Brighton and Third leaned back on their arms, Tyrick and the Investigator rested their elbows on their knees. They heard the soft crunch of the school sandals on the footpath getting louder. Their visitor didn't move terribly quickly but soon enough Professor bol Win came into view.

"Ah," the professor said as he came across the agents of the law.

The Investigator nodded to him. "Professor," she said. "How are you today?"

Bol Win smiled strangely. It seemed too cheerful to the Investigator and there was something behind his eyes. "Very well," he said. "I had hoped to find you out here."

Third looked sideways at him. "Yes?" said the Investigator.

"Yes," said bol Win. "I believe I have cracked your case."

Now all four turned to look at him. The Investigator kept a blank face. "Please," she said, nodding to him.

"You won't like the answer," said bol Win, staring at her. She noticed he wasn't blinking.

"Whatever help you can give will be appreciated."

Bol Win chuckled. "It's not help," he said. "It's the answer." Third rolled his eyes discreetly. Professor bol Win turned his stare on Third. "You're dead."

Third stared back, unfazed. "Am I now?" he said. Bol Win smiled. "Are you threatening me?"

Bol Win shook his head, still smiling. "It's no threat. You're dead. You all are. We all are."

"I don't think I follow you," said the Investigator.

"An infinite number of monkeys," said bol Win.

"Okay," said Third. "Is he drunk?"

"An infinite number of monkeys," bol Win repeated. "On an infinite number of typewriters."

"Of what?"

"Or..." said bol Win. "A handful of monkeys in an infinite amount of time."

The Investigator narrowed her eyes examining the professor in front of them. He stood, his hands in his sleeves, with a gloating look on his face. The expression on his face was too victorious. It was too natural. Whatever this idea was, he truly believed it. "An infinite amount of time?" she asked.

"Have you investigated many plagiarism cases before?"

"A few," said the Investigator.

"Any like this?"

"No."

"And yet here you are," said bol Win, pulling a hand out of a sleeve and making a flourish. "Here you are," he repeated.

"Here we are," said the Investigator, confused but on edge.

"Any other plagiarism case taken you this long?"

"Not that I can recall," said the Investigator.

"No," said bol Win. "So what would it take for you to be here? What would it take for you to have been called out here and to not be able to solve this case? It would have to be something remarkable."

Now the Investigator let the confusion show on her face. "I don't understand."

"If there was a letter out of place, an errant comma, maybe we could have come up with an explanation on our own. But it's perfect. So perfect that we had to call upon the help of the law where we had failed. This is the only scenario where you would be sitting here right now and it is impossible, is it not?" He rolled his head, closing his eyes. "Impossible," he whispered. "Impossible." His eyes snapped open. "But here you are."

"Where are you going with this, professor?" asked the Investigator, an edge coming to her voice.

"We've been here for eternity," bol Win said flatly. "We've been here and every possible scenario has been able to play itself out. Every instance of plagiarism where we were able to explain it away. And it's been so long that we've forgotten every other time it's happened. And at this moment, this impossible moment, you are here only because this is simply one scenario that can exist in an infinite set of possibilities."

The four stared at the professor in silence. Third finally nodded. "You know, that actually makes sense."

"How on the world does that make sense?" said Brighton.

"It's like your simulation, but instead of that, we're all dead."

Professor bol Win snarled at the two officers. "Banter," he said. "That's all you offer. Pointless chatter that is a bore to everyone around you. But it makes no difference. You are the damned and we are in hell." The professor turned, slipped his feet out of the sandals, and walked away. His steps were noiseless as he tread perfectly across the rocks.

"What just happened?" asked Third.

"Chief," said Brighton. The Investigator turned to him. "That man is unhinged. He needs help." She nodded. "If he did do something to cause the plagiarism, it's possible he isn't even aware of it anymore. It would explain why he didn't show as deceptive during your interview with him." She nodded again. "Could be an infection. Some kind of neurological disorder we haven't encountered yet. Tyrick should examine him."

"Me?"

"You're the closest thing we have to a doctor," said Brighton.

"Someone's got to be trained among the faculty here," said Tyrick.

"The Principal is," the Investigator said quietly, still in thought.

"Then you both should, together. Maybe it's something with his advanced age from when he got the treatment, but if it's breaking down, we need to know about it."

"Are we just going to ignore what he said?" asked Third.

"It didn't mean anything," said Tyrick.

The Investigator stared out across the sea. It didn't mean anything.

Arden and Lin were practicing hapkido outside the greenhouse as Greta raced past. Lin had twisted the other's hand back into an awkward position and Arden dropped to his knee.

"Ach!" Arden groaned. "Now where's she going?" he asked as Greta ran into the greenhouse.

"Zeke's in there," said Lin, helping Arden to his feet.

"Is she?" Arden glanced over, then looked at the younger professor. "You know, everyone violates protocol at some point." Lin raised an eyebrow. "It's not a serious concern."

"I haven't violated protocol."

Arden laughed. "I know. Everybody knows. But you should." Lin frowned. "Why haven't you?"

His frown deepened. "I came here..." he paused. "I came here to find some calm. Peace. It wasn't..." he paused again, feeling his chest tighten. "I needed... I also needed..." he paused again.

"Hey, I'm sorry," Arden said. "You don't have to get into it." He clapped Lin on the shoulder. "Spar?"

Lin nodded once, curtly.

The two fought in short, sharp movements. Lin's hands were quicker, cutting past Arden's guard, striking, blocking, redirecting. But he was distracted and a high kick left him stumbling backward. Arden pressed and for a moment had an advantage, but the training activated in Lin, as it always did. He slipped to his left, releasing a jab with his right hand. Arden was stepping forward and caught it squarely on the chin. He blinked once and his feet slipped out from under him. Lin heard the crack before he saw how Arden's arm had bent in a direction it shouldn't.

Lin cursed softly. "I'm sorry."

Arden's face pulled tight in pain but he let out a laugh. He sat up, cradling his left arm, which dangled unnaturally. "Bad luck." Lin knelt down next to him. "Not even sure what happened."

"Is the bone out?"

"No, but it sure wanted to find some daylight. Just a break," Arden added.

"Would you like an analgesic?"

Arden jerkily shook his head. "It'd be fine by the time you got back. Just... I don't know. Distract me. What did you need?"

"What?"

"You needed calm or peace. And something else. Ahhh! What was it?" He closed his eyes, still grimacing.

Lin watched the pain dance over his face. He sighed and looked up at the sky. "I needed order," he said. "After the wars stopped, I didn't have that structure. I didn't do well."

"No? Get into some scrapes?"

"Some," said Lin, thinking back, trying to recall what his days had been like. How he had even survived from one day to the next. "I suppose." Everything was hazy. "I don't really remember. But it wasn't healthy."

"So you came here?"

"Training first. I had to learn how to be a teacher."

Arden gently repositioned his arm, gritting his teeth. He tried to flex his fingers. "Why teaching?" he groaned.

"I heard about the program here," said Lin. "It sounded like..." He thought for a moment. "It sounded like a place to help out and get away."

"Hm," Arden grunted. "Certainly a place to get away." He squeezed down on his forearm.

Lin nodded. "And the rules help. They give me some guidance."

"Doesn't mean you can't have fun," said Arden, slowly

rotating the arm.

Lin nodded again. "I don't need that kind of fun," he said, quietly. "I like what Zeke and I have."

Arden sighed, making a fist and extending his fingers several times rapidly. He stood up, fully moving the healed arm back and forth. "To each their own."

"Sorry about the arm."

"Don't worry about it."

"You can break mine if you like."

"Really?" Arden laughed. Lin shrugged. "Would you even feel anything?"

"Not in the same way," Lin said. "Honestly, no. Not really." Arden laughed again. "Sorry." Lin watched Arden make a little bit too much of a show in testing out his previously broken limb. Arden's gaze kept falling back on Lin's own arm. "Would you like to?" Lin asked again.

Another laugh, but forced. He looked up at Lin. "I don't..." he said. "That's..." He shook his head. "Really?" This time there was a fascination and a hopefulness in the question.

Lin sat down and leaned to his side, propping his arm out straight and lodging his hand between two rocks, rotating his shoulder so that the elbow pointed to the sky. He looked up at Arden. "If you want to."

Lin studied the process that played out on Arden's face, watching every muscle twitch and facial expression, where the eyes darted to, the internal battle that showed itself clearly. Every thought was telegraphed. There was the initial sense that he was supposed to say no, that of course he wouldn't break someone's arm, let alone his colleague. He had to play the part of pretending as if he didn't want to. The eyes moved around too quickly though and bounced too often back to Lin's arm, perfectly vulnerable. The smile that was meant to show that he was a good person who wouldn't do such a thing was just like a mask taped to his face, right below the nose. It didn't extend to his eyes. And then the transition, timed as early as he dared. He wanted to break Lin's arm but he didn't want to seem like he was eager to do it. It was just a fun little experiment. And he had permission, didn't he? It wasn't like he was hurting some innocent person. And it wouldn't hurt anyway. Lin had said so. But he still couldn't seem eager. Play it off, like he could take it or leave it. Break it or not. The shrug, the nonchalant down-turned face. Finally, ask if Lin was sure.

"Are you sure?"

The two stared at each other. Arden, his heart beating faster, the temptation of snapping someone's arm almost overwhelming him. His own bone breaking completely forgotten. Lin, his face flat and calm, having just caught a glimpse of Arden that he knew the other teacher kept care to stay hidden.

The pause drew itself out and a sliver of panic crept onto Arden's face. Would he say no?

Lin nodded once. "Sure."

Relief and joy flashed quickly across Arden's face and another nervous laugh. Then he stepped closer to Lin and slowly raised his foot. Lin kept his eyes on Arden's face.

Behind him, the greenhouse door opened and Zeke and Greta emerged. Arden lowered his foot quickly and turned to face them. Zeke spoke something to Greta, who walked away, and then Zeke approached the two professors.

"What are you up to?" she asked.

"Oh, just sparring," Arden said, too loudly.

Zeke looked down at Lin, who smiled up at her. "What are you doing down there?"

"Working on ground techniques."

"On the rocks?" she said. Lin shrugged. "No, thank you."

"What was Greta after?" Lin asked. Zeke looked

concerned. "Everything okay?"

"Yes," she said slowly. "She's just... I don't know." She stared at Greta's retreating back. "Those kids are getting worked up about something."

Arden looked over. "Do you know what?"

Zeke hesitated. "They're convinced that there's some secret library," she said. Arden and Lin both looked surprised. She shook her head. "And they think bol Win is the culprit." Arden barked a laugh. Lin frowned.

"Is that why they're following him?" Lin asked.

"Following him?" Arden said.

"Yes," said Lin. "They've been shadowing him for a few days now."

Zeke looked down at him. "Why didn't you say anything?"

Lin shrugged. "Since I've been here, they've done it to every one of us at one time or another."

"What?" Arden was startled.

Lin smiled. "You know their spy games."

"Well, they're certainly on the case here," said Zeke. "But I've never seen her like this before. She's absolutely certain of it. Does that sound like her?" she asked, looking to Lin. He shook his head.

"What are you going to do?" asked Arden.

Zeke sighed and looked helpless. "I guess I'll tell the Investigator." Lin stood up, dusting himself off. "Better to say too much than too little."

"I have a meeting set up to get an update for the Principal," said Arden. "I can bring it up with her then, if you would like."

"Oh, I can tell her," said Zeke. The three started to walk back toward the school.

"Still doesn't make much sense," said Lin. "So he reads this secret version of Carmilla, then starts to copy it?"

"Apparently he's still saying that he didn't see it," said

Zeke. "And Greta believes him."

"Can I talk to her about it?" asked Lin.

"Why couldn't you?" asked Arden. "She's your student." Lin waited for Zeke.

"She asked me to keep it secret, but I told her I couldn't do that," said Zeke. "It's fine," she said to Lin. He nodded.

"Doesn't answer why he would be copying it," said Arden.

"A roundabout way of exposing the..." Zeke searched for the right word. "Librarian?"

"Hm."

"How long has the Investigator been here?" asked Lin.

"Seems like forever."

The three continued on to the school. When they reached the west outer door, Arden paused. "Let's just keep this between us," he said. "I mean..." he added quickly, when Zeke looked concerned. "Tell the Investigator of course, but not the other faculty. I'll let the Principal know, but we should leave it at that."

Zeke nodded. "We don't want it getting back to bol Win."

"Right," said Arden. "Especially if..." he stopped.

"If what?" asked Lin.

"If it's true," said Zeke.

The Principal walked briskly down the hall, his arms full of books. He smiled brightly at Max who was sweeping. "Good lad," he said, passing the boy, as Max wore a look of surprised confusion.

The Principal had a clear goal in front of him; something measurable. Not just maintaining the current situation, not just surviving to face another day the same as the one before it. But he needed to think and plan and, most of all, more important than anything else, keep moving forward. The stagnation of the age had settled heavily upon his school and he felt it on his own shoulders. There had been plans once he had first become Principal but they had eventually faded. Any innovations he had implemented slowly deteriorated back into the way that things had been before.

His predecessor had checked in from time to time afterwards, but those became few and far between. The Principal hadn't heard from the previous one for several cycles now. He tried to think back to their conversations. There had been some pride, he remembered, in discussing what he thought were improvements. A sense of embarrassment also, in the idea that the former Principal hadn't been up to the task, hadn't put in place these changes that were clearly better.

What had her name been? Ahir, wasn't it? She had been polite, listened with interest, provided suggestions without trying to undermine his ideas. But she had known then. Known that he was simply following the same pattern that she had. He hadn't realized it at the time, of course, but she knew that his grand vision would ultimately turn back into the way things were.

Not this time. Please, not this time. This time had to be different. For whatever reason, the spark had been lit, and there was no more time to waste. That's all they did now, because it was so easy to waste something that you had an unlimited amount of. But it was no way to live. He felt it, like a weight, crushing down on him, bearing away any motivation he had to struggle. It was so easy to simply exist for one day, because the next was guaranteed. And maybe the next day wouldn't be quite as good as the first. Maybe the sense of purpose would be just a bit more diminished. Maybe the joy of a fresh loaf of bread would be that much less, knowing that it was almost exactly the same as the one before it. Maybe all those things were true, but the difference from one day to the next was so small that it hardly mattered.

If he could compare this day to his first as Principal, what would he think? Each tiny difference from day to day had compounded over an enormous amount of time. He would not have tolerated one moment of the entire day that he totally accepted now.

The Principal walked into his office, dropping the stack of books onto his desk. A cold mug of tea was almost knocked over, and he picked it up and took a sip, making a face at the temperature. He stared at the cup in his hand, as if seeing it for the first time. A knock at the door brought him back to the present and Arden stepped into the room.

The Investigator stared at the boy in front of her yet again. He still looked small. There was more of a presence behind his eyes this time, more defiance, more combativeness. More of a spark. Zeke sat next to him again. "Geoffrey," the Investigator said. He didn't respond but kept staring directly back at her. There was a pause while the Investigator skipped over several questions in her head that she knew were just routine. "Where did you lose sight of Professor bol Win?" she asked finally.

The boy looked surprised at the question. He hadn't realized how much she already knew. "At the edge of the courtyard. The north side," he said.

"You were at the edge of the courtyard?" she asked. He nodded. "But where was he?"

"Oh," he said. "He was walking toward the outer path. But," he added. "He was going at an odd angle. It was kind of..." he paused, thinking. "... a little diagonal to the left. To the west, I mean. North-north-west," he said. He looked at Zeke. "Is that right?"

Before Zeke could respond, the Investigator interjected. "Why do you think he was going that way?"

"I don't know," said Geoffrey.

"You know this place better than I do," said the

Investigator. "What do you think? Why would you walk that way, if you were going to?"

Geoffrey looked down at the table, his eyes scanning back and forth. He looked up. "I would walk that way if I wanted to not leave footprints. Or if I was going to Bear Rock."

"Bear rock?"

"It's a big rock that looks like a bear. It's off the side of the outer path, on the outside, by about thirty meters."

"What about the footprints?"

"There are bigger rocks the way he was going. You don't leave footprints on that like in the dust or even the gravel."

Now the Investigator looked surprised, while a small smile came over Zeke. The Investigator looked at her, and the professor shrugged. "They take hide-and-seek very seriously," Zeke said.

"It's not hide-and-seek," said Geoffrey. "It's free-me."

"Close enough. Don't contradict."

The Investigator shook her head. "Alright," she said. "How long were you out there?"

Geoffrey shrugged. "Not long," he said. "Just a minute or two, I guess. I didn't want to be there when he came back."

"Did you see or hear anything strange when you were going back to the student quarters?" Geoffrey shook his head. "What was on the note?" Geoffrey looked down at the table again but his eyes were still. "Geoffrey." He stayed quiet. The Investigator leaned back in her chair.

"It was a lie," he said, very quietly.

"What?"

"It was a lie," he said, louder. "I didn't know what else to do. I'm sorry." He looked up at Zeke with a pained expression on his face. She patted his arm.

"It's alright, Geoff," she said. "Just tell her what you wrote."

He turned back to the Investigator with an ashamed look. "It said I know about the books."

The Investigator nodded. "Anything else?" Geoffrey shook his head. The Investigator thought for a moment, then looked at Zeke. "Can you identify their hand-writing?" Zeke nodded. The Investigator looked back at Geoffrey. "Did you think of that? Wouldn't he have known you wrote it?"

He shook his head. "I traced it. From another book."

"Another book? What book?"

"Dracula."

"A sentence like that isn't in Dracula," said Zeke.

"No, I just traced each word separate."

The Investigator snorted a laugh. "Criminal masterminds," she muttered. "Well," she said. "Any other intelligence acquired from following your target?" she asked, playfully. Geoffrey solemnly shook his head. "Geoffrey," the Investigator said. "I need to know if you've ever seen this secret library."

He looked startled. "No," he said quickly. "I swear." She stared at him without speaking. "Honestly! I've never seen it."

"Have you ever seen an unofficial copy of Carmilla?" the Investigator asked.

"No!" he said.

"Even if we find this library," the Investigator said. "We still don't have an answer to how you plagiarized." The boy winced at the word. "Can you tell me anything about that?"

He looked helpless again. "I don't know," he pleaded. "I don't know how it happened."

The Investigator was silent for a moment. "Okay," she said. "Why don't you give me a moment with Professor Zeke." Geoffrey stood up. "And Geoffrey," said the Investigator. "Stop following Professor bol Win." He looked down. "All of you. You understand?" He nodded slowly, and walked out.

The two women watched him go. Once the door had closed, Zeke looked to the Investigator, expectantly.

The Investigator was quiet. What an absurd case this was

turning into. It had started off strange and only gotten worse. There were no clear answers to anything that she needed to know. She closed her eyes, wishing she could just go home. Taking a deep breath, she opened her eyes again. "Is it possible for a professor to mentally manipulate a student to the point where they could copy something word for word?"

Zeke leaned back and frowned. "That would be..." she paused. "... extraordinarily difficult."

"Is it possible?"

"I..." she sighed. "I don't know. I'm not an expert in the kind of neurological development that would require."

"Does anyone here have that kind of expertise?"

Zeke looked uncomfortable. "Professor bol Win." She leaned back. "But it doesn't make any sense. Why would he want to do that?"

The Investigator rubbed her forehead. "Right now, we're just trying to figure out how this could be done."

"Everyone's a suspect, is that it?"

"Something like that."

Zeke stared at her. "I should be too, right? I'm his mentor, after all." The Investigator gave a sympathetic shrug. Zeke snorted. "Well, thank you for not lying to me anyway."

The Investigator gave a small laugh. "I might have if I thought it would have worked." And Zeke laughed too.

"Can I..." Zeke stopped. "I'd like to ask you something else," she said. "Not really related to the investigation. So it doesn't matter if I'm a suspect, right?" She smiled, trying to clarify the joke. The Investigator raised an eyebrow, presumably because she recognized it wasn't truly a joke. Zeke sighed. The library room was quiet. Like Geoffrey and the other children, Zeke had spent much time in this room and the others like it, diving deep into distant lands and new ideas. She had always felt like the room was limitless, its simplicity allowing it to expand infinitely based on whatever she was reading. But now it just felt small and stuffy. "The children," she said. "Where do they come from?"

The Investigator placed her palms flat on the table. "Why do you ask?"

Zeke sighed again, deeply. "There's so much I don't know," she said. "So much about this boy that is a mystery, to me and to him. He doesn't remember his past. He doesn't know anything about where he came from. Please."

The Investigator slid her hands back and into her lap. "What has the Principal told you?" she asked. She didn't bother asking if Zeke had ever made this inquiry to the Principal. Of course she had.

Zeke looked uncomfortable. "He said it's best not to know. That it doesn't matter anyway, and it could affect how I treat him. How we treat them," she corrected. "It's the same with all the other students and mentors."

"Hm." The Investigator processed that.

"That was..." Zeke looked up, trying to do the calculations in her head, then gave up. "... cycles ago. Shortly after I arrived. What difference does it make?"

The Investigator pursed her lips. "Have you tried asking him again?" she said.

"No." Zeke pinched the bridge of her nose.

The two sat there in silence. The Investigator working through in her head what she should do, the professor waiting to find out the verdict. Not long ago, the Investigator might have sat there without speaking for a longer time. But she knew what she was going to do immediately and there was no point in dragging it out, even though that was her instinct.

"The report I have..." the Investigator said. Zeke looked up quickly. "... states that the children are orphans." Zeke nodded; she knew that part. "The rest..." the Investigator hesitated.

Zeke interrupted in the pause. "It never made sense to me

that they were orphans. Longevity treatments had been around for centuries. Death rates had dropped to practically nothing. How could there be that many orphans of all roughly the same age? It's remarkable that there were even that many children at the same time. Population controls had been in place for quite a while."

The Investigator nodded slowly. She became aware that she was wringing her hands. In these moments, she felt the cruelty of the universe. "They were test subjects, but they were also the children of test subjects," she said. "Tests that did not go well." The air fell heavy around them. "There was a focus on reversing the effects of the treatment."

"Reversing?" Zeke said. "Why?"

The Investigator shrugged. "It wasn't nefarious. To give people more control over their lives," she said. "Didn't you feel anxiety about when to get the treatment?" Zeke nodded. "So maybe you get it when you're twenty-five and after a few cycles you decide to age up a bit. Give yourself some more brain development." She was still wringing her hands. "They were also trying to reverse the aging process. Again, just more control. As you can imagine, it didn't work. It was the attempts at reversal that killed the most number of subjects." Zeke blinked at the sudden revelation. "At the time, there was a belief that cells from the children of the subjects would help with the de-aging. I have no idea how." The Investigator frowned. "But the recruited subjects all had children. When the parents had died, someone had the bright idea of continuing the research on the children." Zeke inhaled sharply. The Investigator looked up at the ceiling. She wished there was a window she could be staring out of right now and not have this feeling of being trapped in the small room. "They were slightly more cautious," she said, darkly. "And only a few died." Zeke was very quiet. "It was decided that the rest would be spared, but they had nothing to do with them.

Nowhere to put them. So they concocted the idea of using them to create art."

The room was quiet again until Zeke broke the silence. "I thought they were always intended to be artists," she said softly. The Investigator shook her head. "Our whole purpose here," Zeke said. "It was just an afterthought?" The Investigator couldn't respond. "What?" Tears sprang into Zeke's eyes. "What am I doing here? What are any of us doing here?"

The Investigator reached across the table and took Zeke's hand. "You're safeguarding these children," she said firmly.

"For how long?" Zeke asked, wildly. "For what? What are we doing here?" she insisted. "How long have I been here? How long have I been protecting someone else's mistake?"

The Investigator held onto her hand tighter. "Listen to me," she said. "Listen. There is a world past these walls that has fallen into decay," the Investigator said, staring into Zeke's face. She saw the anxiety rushing through the teacher's eyes and tried to draw it out. "I travel from planet to planet, from star to star, and I see the same things. I see mining operations digging deeper and deeper holes into any rock we can find. I see people living in palaces with the same vacant expressions on all their faces. You have something here. You have a purpose."

"What purpose?" Zeke choked out.

"You are caring for these children. No one else would. How long have you been here? Since before the wars?" Zeke nodded. "Did you know you were almost incinerated?"

Tears were still slowly creeping down Zeke's face. She shook her head. "We knew it was a possibility," she said quietly.

"It was more than just a possibility. It was barely prevented during the Lunar Siege. The entire planet was almost obliterated." Zeke looked up in faint surprise. "That's classified, by the way. Don't tell anyone," the Investigator said, as an afterthought. "You wouldn't have even known it was happening. You probably would have noticed the rumbling, probably chalked it up to a minor earthquake. Then a wall of fire would have engulfed you before you even knew what direction it was coming from. And no one else in this universe would have spared a thought for you or for these children."

"Why are you saying this?" Zeke gasped.

"Because," the Investigator sat back sharply, angry. "Because out there is rotten. This is the first place I've been to with decency since..." she stopped, thinking. "A long time. I want you to know that what you're doing is good," she said, looking back to Zeke. "It's good. You should be proud of the work you're doing. I promise you, it's the only worthwhile effort going on right now."

"Will it keep going?"

"What?" The Investigator stared at the defiant eyes looking back at her.

"The faculty," Zeke said. "They're worried this incident will cause the school to be closed."

"Closed? How..." she trailed off.

"That if a student has been found to have plagiarized, Central Authority will cancel the program outright. Close the school down and re-home the children."

"Oh."

There was a moment of silence.

"Is that a valid fear?" Zeke asked.

The Investigator didn't reply. She looked back at Zeke with an expressionless face.

"I see," Zeke said.

"I can't answer that question."

"I believe you just did."

"No." The Investigator sighed. "I couldn't answer it either

way."

"Why not?" Zeke stared at her. "You told me about where the children came from. Why not this? How is this worse?" The Investigator was silent. "Can we just not do this? Can we not have the moment where you sit there knowing something that I don't know? Can you just tell me? Please!"

The last word came out louder than she had intended. The Investigator startled up, standing, stammering. "I'm sorry," she whispered, making for the door.

Zeke was out of her chair in a moment too, grasping the Investigator's hands, coming closer than she had intended. "Wait," she said.

The two stood inches apart. Zeke realized they were still holding hands, thought about releasing them, stepping back. She stayed where she was. The room felt much smaller.

"Central doesn't know what to do with these children," the Investigator said, softly. "They never have. I can't tell you what they'll do next. I don't know."

"But..." Zeke frowned. "So it is a valid fear."

The Investigator shrugged. Zeke felt her hands rise and fall slightly at the same time. "It's a possibility every day. It's been a possibility every day before this one. It doesn't have anything to do with Geoffrey." Now Zeke felt the Investigator's hands tighten, squeezing hers ever so softly. "I have to go," the Investigator said quietly.

Zeke nodded as the Investigator slipped out of the room.

EIGHT

THE COLLAPSE

Tyrick and Third lazily followed Brighton as he slowly walked the north edge of the courtyard. He turned off, carefully picking his way across the rocks, staring intently at the ground. The other two hung back slightly, but disinterestedly continued to shadow him.

"Bear Rock," said Third.

"Mm," said Tyrick.

"I saw a bear once."

"Mmhmm."

"I did! It was on a science moon or something. You know, the ones they used for repopulating."

"You were stationed there?"

"It was a protection detail."

"Protection against what?"

"Bears." The two laughed. "Smugglers. Back when that was a concern."

Brighton carefully made his way to another rock. The boy hadn't been wrong. Footprints were virtually nonexistent on these rocks. Any sand or dust transfer was almost entirely scraped clean by the wind. He bent down and sniffed a rock. It seemed like he was on the trail.

"Any run-ins with smugglers?"

"Not there, but I did on some trade routes."

Tyrick shook his head. "What was the point? They weren't stealing anything they couldn't get legally."

Third shrugged. "Habit, I guess. It was the only thing they knew. Wasn't it..." he waved a hand, trying to find the right word. "...hard, after everyone stopped killing each other?"

Tyrick wagged his head back and forth. "It was a little strange."

Brighton imagined the dark, only starlight to see by. Where would he step to avoid slipping? Where would he place his foot to stay silent? There wasn't any reason that bol Win had to think he was being followed, but it was human nature while acting surreptitiously. He would have been sneaking about while he was sneaking about. Trying to stay quiet even though there was no rational reason to do so. Sound out here fell flat. The professor could have driven a rock crawler and not been heard. But hopefully he went in a straight line. Brighton felt pretty confident he had the bearing, but the signs had dried up.

"What was it like?" Third asked, emphasizing the second word.

Tyrick stepped carefully over the rocks. "It was..." he paused, thinking back. "I don't even know. You know," he said. "I listened to all these interviews of soldiers. There was a lot of news coverage, obviously, after the last peace accords."

"I've seen some."

"The ones where they were all lost and everything. No purpose and all that. And I just remember thinking that's how I was supposed to feel." Third waited for him to go on. "I don't know. I didn't feel much of anything."

"That's a little strange, isn't it?" Third said. "I'd feel relief."

Tyrick shook his head. "The conditioning was intense. Any sense of relief was going up against about a hundred years of people drilling into your head that battle was glorious. I guess it all just canceled itself out for me."

"Hm."

"You know what I felt? I felt confused because I didn't know what I was going to do next. That's it. I didn't know how I was going to live. They didn't teach us how to be in polite society."

Third laughed. "Is that what we are?"

"More polite than a squad of soldiers."

Brighton had reached the outer path. He surveyed it carefully. Glancing up, he looked for what the boy had called Bear Rock. There was a large rock ahead, but it didn't look much like a bear to him. He had hoped to find a footfall in the gravel path that cut across it, perpendicular to the normal traffic that would be on it. Someone would have to take at least two steps to clear it, and probably three. He knelt down and sniffed again.

"What do you think he smells?" asked Third.

"Feet." The two laughed.

Third looked around. "That repopulation moon? There were trees and plants and waterfalls. And obviously animals. They had a bunch set up in the same system for different time periods." He shook his head. "I've never seen so many different living things all at once, you know? Not like this wreck." Tyrick chuckled. "This place is a nightmare. Imagine living here."

"Is that supposed to be Bear Rock?" Tyrick jerked his head at the large rock past Brighton.

"I guess. Looks like a bear's ass from this angle."

"You're the expert on the fauna," said Tyrick, clapping him on the shoulder. "Let's see if Brighton knows what he's doing."

The two approached Brighton, who was still crouched down by the footpath. He looked discouraged. "Anything?" asked Third.

"This terrain is horrible," said Brighton. "I can't be sure. If I had to guess..." he paused. "He crossed here, heading for the rock. But I don't know if that's just because of what the kid said. It would have been better to not have the suggestion."

"Well," said Tyrick. "We'll keep you in the dark next time. Let's check out the rock."

"Company," Third said quietly.

Arden was approaching on the path, his sandals crunching on the gravel. He pulled up noticeably when he saw the officers, but recovered and continued walking toward them. "Hello," he said, casually. The three nodded in reply and Tyrick returned the spoken greeting. The wind softly whistled through the rocks providing the only sound while the four men stood in an awkward moment. "Out for a stroll?" Arden said.

Tyrick caught the barely disguised edge on the professor's voice. "Yes," he said.

The question and answer hung in the air, ridiculously. Arden looked from one officer to the next, each one keeping an impassive face. "How's the investigation going?" he asked, finally.

"Oh, we're mostly just trying to stay out of the way," said Tyrick. "The Investigator is doing all the work."

Arden nodded. "You must have some ideas though," he said. "What do you think happened?"

Tyrick shrugged. "Couldn't say, really. What about you? You have a much better idea of the place." The careful redirection worked.

Arden grunted and crossed his arms, unconsciously assuming the same pose he used when teaching a class. "It's so unusual," he said. "We've obviously never seen anything like this." Tyrick murmured, trying to keep him going. "If I had to guess," Arden said. "I would say that it was a repressed memory. He read the story somehow in the past and it's resurfaced in this way." Tyrick murmured again, nodding. "We really don't know everything that can happen in the brain over these kinds of time periods," Arden continued. "We weren't meant to live this long, you know."

"So they tell me," Tyrick said.

"Think about it, can you remember what you were doing,"

Arden shrugged. "Fourteen cycles ago?" He looked directly at Third.

Third nodded. "Absolutely. I wasn't alive fourteen cycles ago."

Arden laughed. "Five cycles then."

"Nope."

"How old are you?" Arden asked, with what seemed to be a feigned surprise to Tyrick.

"He's a baby," said Brighton.

Arden was carefully looking at Third, who stared steadily back, unperturbed. Tyrick wasn't sure of the point of Arden's prying. He didn't care for it, but he also wanted to see more of where Arden was going with it, and stayed silent.

"One cycle?" Arden asked. "Have you been around when the Dante and Virgil dock?"

Third didn't even blink. "Nope," he said again.

Now Arden's eyes shifted to Brighton and Tyrick. His whole body posture had changed. His head was angled down, and he was leaning slightly back, as if in a defensive posture. It was as though he expected Third to attack him at any moment. "He's the latest version, isn't he?" Arden said.

"That's rude," Third said. "I'm standing right here."

Arden looked back to him, and his eyes narrowed. "What's the point of you?" he asked. "A new breed of super soldier."

"I'm not a soldier," Third said flatly. He glanced at Tyrick. "No offense." Tyrick smiled.

"Why is Central even spending the resources to develop someone like you?" Arden asked. Third slowly turned his head back to Arden. Tyrick could see his junior officer bristling, in his own way. There was a calmness that settled over him as his heart rate dropped to almost nothing and his breathing stopped entirely. He'd never attack the professor, of course, but he had triggered the physiological response anyway. Arden didn't seem to notice. "We're out here on the edge of the world, forgotten, and they're still focused on building weapons," Arden said, resentfully. "Why is that?"

"Officer Third brings an incredibly valuable set of skills and abilities to our team," Tyrick said, calmly. "I'm sure you can recognize the need for formidable bodies in deep space environments. Even soldiers are susceptible to the harsh conditions in which we are trying to expand." His voice was toneless, as if he was simply reciting, which wasn't far from the truth.

"And if some of those expanding colonies decide they want to go their own way, he's also got an incredibly valuable set of skills and abilities for keeping them in line, doesn't he?" Arden spat out. Tyrick didn't respond, simply continued to look at Arden as the anger radiated off of the professor's body. "Expand," Arden scoffed. His anger hadn't yet dissipated. "Expand to what? And why? We're just killing time here anyway. That's all we're left with." He glared at the three officers. "Excuse me," he muttered, and stalked past them.

"What an angry young man," Third said, as the professor disappeared from view. He had resumed breathing.

Tyrick sighed. "Come on," he said. "Let's check out this rock."

The Investigator found the Principal in the kitchen, peeling potatoes. He was strangely energetic, considering his task. She saw his head bouncing slightly back and forth, as if to a tune in his head. His feet were shuffling a little as well. She smiled.

"Good afternoon," she said.

"Ah!" he turned over his shoulder and smiled at her. "And how are you?" He was standing at a prepping table in the middle of the room. The Investigator slowly walked around to the other side, marveling a bit at the size of the mound of potatoes in front of the head of the school.

"Is that befitting your station?" she asked. The Principal laughed. "Surely this is a job for the children."

"Only as a punishment," the Principal said.

"What crime did you commit to incur this sentence?"

The Principal laughed again. "I don't mind peeling potatoes, you know," he said. "But I feel delighted to be doing so right now." The Investigator raised her eyebrows. "I can't explain it," the Principal said. He picked up another potato, inspecting it in his hand. "That's not true," he said, almost to himself. "I absolutely can explain it. Isn't that odd?" He looked up at his guest. She leaned back against a cupboard. "I've got one of those bursts of energy," the Principal said. "I've got," he stopped. "A few days ago, I came to a decision. I have decided to direct my efforts at reinvigorating the creative spark that has faded to an almost imperceptible glimmer in humanity." The Investigator smiled at the formal but playful tone. The Principal nodded. "The original mission of the school. That's what we came here for, and that's what I am going to carry out. We are going to send our work out into the world, into the," he waved. "The universe!"

"Are the children ready?" the Investigator asked. The Principal scoffed.

"Of course not!" he said. "They're children!" The Principal set the potato and the peeler down on the table. "It didn't take long for us, once this school was up and running, to see that we had made a terrible mistake." He looked downcast at the memory, then continued. "We had been fooling ourselves, thinking that we could somehow mine the creativity out of children. It was ghoulish. So most of us quickly turned to the goal of creating a reasonable life for them."

"Were there any attempts to get them back around other people?" the Investigator interrupted.

"There was. Not with these kids. One of the other schools. It didn't turn out well. It just," he shook his head. "Society wasn't designed for perpetual children to be running around. So we kept them to the original plan on paper. But really, it was just to give them some decent quality of life."

"What's changed?"

"Hm?"

"If you know it's a mistake to mine them," she asked, using the Principal's term. "How are you going to return to the original mission?"

He smiled and picked up the peeler again and waved it for emphasis. "We had initially planned to train the children and when they were ready, begin to publish their original work. But their work is fairly rubbish." The Investigator stifled a laugh. "I mean, it's passable. But they're children. The notion of the child genius is just a fancy. We should have realized that from the beginning. Great works of literature, or any art, they take skill and craft and work. They take development. And we've cut these poor children off from that. They can't grow. Not into adulthood, and not as writers." He looked sad. "Ever. That's the worst part," he said, frowning. "But," he announced. "That's no excuse. We've got to get out there!" He waved the peeler to the ceiling.

"Out there?" the Investigator couldn't help but ask.

"To everyone! To the stars, to the cities. We're going," he said, softly but firmly.

"Who is going?"

"Whoever wants to," the Principal said. "Children and faculty."

"But," the Investigator looked confused. "Go where?"

The Principal laughed. "Long ago, artists would travel, bringing their work with them, putting on demonstrations and exhibitions. That's what we are going to do."

"And the children are the spark?" she asked.

"Yes," the Principal said, stabbing the peeler into the table. "Exactly. They aren't creating the great works. They are demonstrating the possibilities. The artists are out there, just waiting."

The Investigator was silent, imagining it all. A spaceship of kids and teachers, settling down on a terraforming planet, reading their work to crowds. Could they pull them away from the holo-vids and drugs? That would be something to see, in any case. She nodded once to the Principal. "I like your plan," she said simply.

He inclined his head in a small bow. "Thank you," he said.

"It doesn't help me that much at the moment."

The Principal laughed, ashamed. "No, I suppose it doesn't."

"But it's a good plan," she said. "I'm glad you have it. I'm glad you," she paused. "I'm glad you found this purpose."

The Principal beamed at the sincerity, and nodded again at the Investigator. He frowned suddenly. "Do you know what I'm most afraid of?" The Investigator looked questioningly. "I'm afraid of losing it before I can get it off the ground, so to speak. This feeling I have right now. I know it's temporary. This kind of energy always is. It can't last forever. I have to see this through, and I'm so scared of falling back into the same routine. The same patterns as before. Just existing." He looked directly at the Investigator. "It terrifies me."

She nodded. "What can stop you?" she asked.

"Only me," he said. "That's what scares me most of all. If I fail, it will be on my head alone."

"Well," she said. "Get some friends. People who will hold you to it. You're part of the original generation, right?" The Principal nodded. "I don't know what that's like," the Investigator said. "I don't know what it was like to have a body that I thought was going to fail in a hundred different ways."

The Principal laughed slightly. "But you've got a machine there," she pointed at his chest. "That is an unstoppable force. I could jam that potato peeler into your heart, and you'd be okay." He looked down with some surprise at the peeler still in his hand. "You can always keep moving forward, no matter what. You can tell your arms and legs to take you wherever you want to go. Remember that." The Investigator stopped and looked around the kitchen. She picked up a tomato and sniffed it. "I hope we won't be here much longer. I don't want to delay you. But I will miss this place."

Greta wiped the window clean, squeezing the cloth into the small bucket on her waist. She was outside in the courtyard, cleaning surfaces. She snuck a glance behind her. Professor bol Win still sat on a rock several meters out. It had a funny shape to it that gave it a natural seat with a back. Professor bol Win sat there many afternoons, contemplating, he said. The children said you could see his butt in the stone. Greta giggled to herself at the thought.

Professor Zeke had told her to stop following Professor bol Win. But it wasn't her fault that she was doing chores here. It wasn't Shinty's fault that he happened to be sweeping while Professor bol Win left his room. It wasn't Lulu's fault that she was working on a story about rocks that came alive, and had to walk outside to get inspiration, just as Professor bol Win would walk the grounds. That was all just a coincidence.

Suddenly, he stood up. Greta frowned. He hadn't been there that long. His contemplations should have just been getting started. She watched as he went further out toward the outer path and then she saw Professor Arden walking along it. Professor bol Win raised his hand, and called out a greeting.

Greta held her breath. The two were fairly far away, and they didn't seem to be paying attention to her. She might be able to get closer if she was quiet. As casually as she could, she stepped away from the windows. This was ridiculous. She was too far away and could never get close without them seeing. Maybe Lulu was around. It was still too early though. They hadn't expected to have to improvise like this. It was up to her. Greta took a deep breath and began to walk out to the path.

What was her cover story? She was exercising. That would be enough to get her onto the path. Then maybe she could get to a rock to hide behind. At the very least, she would be able to hear a snippet of the conversation as she passed them.

"Greta."

She jumped. Professor Lin had entered the courtyard without her noticing. Now he meandered over to her. She gave a furtive look back to Professors bol Win and Arden. What were they talking about?

"How are you?"

"Fine, Professor Lin."

"What are you up to this morning?"

"Cleaning the windows."

"Any windows in that direction?" He nodded his head to the two figures.

Greta flinched. "I'm just thinking through a story!" Greta said, feeling pleased at having come up with an excuse that wasn't technically a lie.

"Oh?" said Professor Lin.

"Yes!"

"What's it about?"

"Well," said Greta. "It's about bees and the creation of wasps." Professor Lin raised an eyebrow. "The bees have terrible wars among them and they go on for generations and generations. Lots of tribes of bees all battling each other." Professor Lin nodded. "Until one day, the evil bee general

Malkalie uses his terrible magic to create an army of monsters to fight for him!" Greta was flourishing her arms this way and that. "A twisted, hideous, unstoppable perversion of a bee. The wasp!" she announced dramatically.

"Oh my goodness," said Professor Lin.

"Yeah!" said Greta. "But they can't be controlled, not even by Malkalie. And soon, they start to overpower all the bee tribes. And the bees have to join together to fight back against the evil wasps."

"The joining together over a common enemy story?"

Greta nodded. "And unchecked power and all that," she said.

"Sounds fun," said Professor Lin. "Why don't you go work on it instead of following Professor bol Win."

"I'm," she started to protest, but she knew it was hopeless. "Sorry," she quietly finished.

"And tell the others," said Professor Lin. "Let him be."

"She wasn't supposed to tell anybody," Greta grumbled.

"Don't blame Professor Zeke," he said. "Now get. Go help out in the kitchen."

"The windows!"

"They'll be there tomorrow."

Lin watched her retreat back to the school. Wasn't that remarkable? None of these children had ever so much as seen an insect, let alone a bee or a wasp. They had only read about them in books. But they were as real to them as anything they encountered in their lives. So real they could imagine new stories and mythologies. The evil bee general Malakie. Malakie? Malkalie, that was it.

He felt a touch of pride at his student.

But what does it say that they still write of war? A cloud passed over his face. It probably says that literature is too replete with war stories. He frowned deeper at the thought of it. Thank the skies and the earth that had ended. He turned and looked out across the rocks. Bol Win and Arden were still talking. He saw bol Win hand something to Arden. It looked like Arden was staring at it. Must be the note. What else could it be?

Lin imagined being told about it by Arden. Would he have to pretend he was hearing about it for the first time? Maybe Arden would tell him to keep it a secret and then he'd have to act surprised the next time he heard about it too. Lin shook his head. The professors here were almost as bad as the children with their cloak and dagger games.

The two men separated, Arden continuing on the path, bol Win walking back toward the school. The elder professor nodded to Lin as he passed him.

Footsteps padded softly in the hall. The two pairs of sandals were identical, apart from size; the larger belonging to a woman, the smaller to a boy no more than ten. They walked purposefully, but not too fast for the boy to have to hurry.

Geoffrey still felt trepidation as he walked to the Principal's office, but it was lessened by having Professor Zeke with him. He glanced out the windows as he passed them, seeing the dusty rocks, looking for each one as it fell out of view from one window and reappeared in the next, the angle just slightly different.

Zeke looked down at the boy as he gazed out the window. She knew he was in his own head, and she smiled. There was a whole world going on between his ears, one that she barely had any access to. It reminded her that this was a unique person, in the same way that she was. It was so easy to think that everyone else was just an object orbiting her own sphere. That they weren't as complicated and contradictory as she herself was. Just simple beings with simple minds. It obviously wasn't true. It helped to be reminded of it.

They arrived at the Principal's door, and she knocked once and went in, holding the door for Geoffrey to follow. The Principal was at his desk, and he stood up as they entered. He smiled. "Come in, come in." Professor Zeke had never seen him so happy as he had been the past several days. "Please," he gestured to the two chairs in front of his desk, and they came and sat. "And how are you today?" he asked, looking at Geoffrey.

"Very well, Principal," said Geoffrey, a little surprised at the enthusiasm. It was a bit different from the last time he was here.

"Good, good," said the Principal. "And you?"

"Very well," echoed Zeke.

"Good, good," the Principal repeated. "Good, good." He stared at the papers in front of him. "You're probably wondering why I've invited you here. What am I saying? Of course you're wondering that. It's the most natural thing in the world, isn't it? Why would I even say that?" Zeke stifled a smile at the verbalized train of thought. "I wanted to talk to you about," he paused. "I should have figured out what I was going to say, shouldn't've I? Shouldn't've. What a word. Should not have I? What a sentence. Makes no sense, doesn't it? Does not it. I've never understood contractions. What a development."

Poor Geoffrey gaped at this unfiltered stream of consciousness.

The Principal laughed. "I wanted to talk to you about the next stage of the school." Now even Zeke looked startled.

"Is this," she began. "Should we discuss this at a faculty conference first?" she asked. Geoffrey stayed perfectly still, barely daring to breathe.

"No, no," said the Principal. "I specifically wanted to talk about it with you two." He looked out the window. "All this business with," he sighed. "The plagiarism." Geoffrey shrunk into his chair. "It's," he paused, his gaze detaching from the view outside and passing into the middle distance. "It's a sign of things, isn't it?" he said softly. He turned back to the other two. "Not something mysterious. But a signal to us. That we need to do better. That we need to do more." Zeke frowned. "I want to go on a field trip," said the Principal.

Geoffrey looked confused. "Outside?" he asked.

The Principal laughed. "You could say that. But I want to go a bit farther."

"The ridge?" asked Geoffrey.

"Have you been to the ridge before?" asked the Principal.

"No, Principal," said Geoffrey. "At least, I don't remember if I have. I don't remember how we came when I first arrived. It must have been that way, though."

"Yes, it was," said the Principal, smiling. "But you were asleep. All the students were. It was nighttime." He closed his eyes, thinking back, so long ago. Then opened them quickly. "But that's the past. We look to the future!" he announced, waving his arm, and delighting the boy.

"Where exactly do you want to go?" asked Zeke.

The Principal took a deep breath. "I want to travel to the other schools, collect as many students and faculty who are interested, and travel the nearby systems putting on exhibitions of the artistry of the individuals at these institutions." That was something he had prepared.

Zeke blinked several times. Geoffrey looked confused.

"Are you interested?" asked the Principal.

"What?" gasped Zeke.

"Are you interested to travel the stars, and showcase the amazing work that you have done here? To visit distant planets and remote space stations. To see the wonders of this universe, and to have your words heard and read by countless individuals who currently sit in the dark? To bring them the light of your talents, and of others like you?"

Zeke sat in silence at the peculiar speech. Waves of emotions crashed over her, one after another. Confusion, followed by fear, followed by curiosity. And then, last of all and most of all, a profound joy mixed with hope. Could this really happen?

Geoffrey sat, still confused. "Can I go?" he asked.

"Of course you can, my lad!" the Principal exclaimed.

"Can Pency?"

"If he chooses to," said the Principal. "This will be strictly voluntary."

"Oh," said Geoffrey. "Okay. I'll go if Pency does."

Zeke laughed with the Principal. "Is this," started Zeke. "Is this really happening?" She was almost breathless.

"Yes," said the Principal, firmly. "Yes," he repeated. "Yes." He looked directly at Zeke. "We are going to do this."

"And what can you deduce from me?"

She had been sitting outside, trying to soak in the new plan that had been laid at her feet, the new adventure. The Investigator had found her there and sat down on the rocks beside.

"From you?" The Investigator turned a careful eye to her, slowly scanning up and down. Zeke watched with a smile on her face. "Let's see. You come from a wealthy family, but you've rejected that life. Turning to this monastic setting might be seen as some kind of penance, but the truth is you simply want to help these children. You've been here about half your life and you have come to love it a great deal. Before this you wasted time at the holo-clubs, never feeling like you fit in. You traveled a bit, even a few forays into the wilderness. Still, this school is the farthest distance you've been from home, which was..." The Investigator paused, contemplating. "Caro Falls."

Zeke let out a delighted laugh. "How on the world did you

guess that? Wait, let me try." She leaned back, still smiling. "The wealth is fairly easy, isn't it? Aesthetic modifications were never cheap and clearly this is unnatural."

"Unnatural?" the Investigator interrupted. "That's a harsh word for it. You don't like them?"

"I... it's a complicated relationship. They are who I am but they were never something I chose. Are not something that I would have ever chosen. It's an uncomfortable feeling, knowing that your body is a marker of wealth and power over others. Like I'm a designer handbag for my parents. They could show they have a perfect apartment, perfect transport, perfect geneticist, perfect trainers, perfect everything, and I'm just a checkbox on that list."

"Hm," the Investigator murmured.

"Where were we?" Zeke said, smiling again. "Obviously I've rejected it all if I'm here. A fair guess to say that I had to waste some time before finding my calling. And I wouldn't have been here for as long as I have been if it wasn't my calling. Oh! And half my life? That's very clever. You knew I'd been here for three cycles and you must have known that this combination of genetics..." She gestured at herself. "... was terribly common about six cycles ago." She gave a victorious smile, then frowned. "But how did you know I was from Caro Falls? The accents there are a complete mishmash of everywhere else. The styles were the same all across that hemisphere. How did you do it? What gave it away?"

The Investigator raised an eyebrow.

"Ah!" Zeke raised her hands. "The necklace!"

"The necklace?"

"Hanging on my wall in my room. You must have seen it as you've been snooping around." Zeke gave a mischievous smile.

"I read your file," the Investigator said, simply.

"What?" Zeke laughed.

"It's all there. I couldn't deduce any of it. Too many variables."

"What do you mean? I just laid it out."

"You laid out the narrative that you knew was correct. There are many other narratives that fit the facts that would still have been wrong. Styles come and go all the time, there's no way to pinpoint when you were born just from how you look. Wealth, fine, but beyond that? Plenty of wealthy people have good relationships with their families, even ones who go off on their own adventures. And it's a beautiful piece of jewelry, but I've seen the like in half a dozen territories."

"But the design is unique to Caro Falls! The jeweler lives there."

"They may very well, but objects travel."

Zeke leaned back. "So that's it? Deduction is a fantasy? Sherlock Holmes is just a character in a story?"

The Investigator shrugged. "It's a good reminder that coming up with a story to fit clues is a fraught exercise. Deduction is quite limited," she said. "But not always out of place."

The two held a stare.

"You were wrong about something," the Investigator said, softly.

"What was that?"

"Your geneticist. They weren't perfect."

"Oh no?" Zeke gave a small laugh.

"No. There is an imperfection in your right eye. A speck of brown that doesn't fit. If it were intentional, it would have been gold and there would have been several. And another imperfection on your left ear. A slight discoloration. It's very difficult to see due to your hair. I only caught it once."

"Maybe it was only a trick of the light."

"Hm," the Investigator murmured. "I doubt it." She lifted a hand. "May I?"

Zeke nodded once. The Investigator's hand gently pushed the hair back behind Zeke's ear, her thumb grazing against the ear lobe.

"And?" Zeke asked, trying to keep her voice level even as she felt her lungs tighten.

"I was right," the Investigator said, simply.

"So," Zeke said, clearing her throat, leaning back, raising her eyebrows. The Investigator's hand fell away from Zeke's ear and the long blond strands came sweeping in to cover it up again. "Now you have seen my imperfections, slight though they may be. Do you find me to be marred beyond hope?"

The Investigator smiled. "I've always thought the beauty in the universe came from its chaos. Its unpredictability. Were every strand of your DNA in its intended place, you would not be nearly so beautiful. Not nearly so perfect."

She walked through the school in a daze. Everything seemed buzzing and alive and far away. She went to her room early and lay in bed, watching the slow-ivy on the ceiling. As the light faded outside, the leaves gradually slipped away into the darkness. In the perfect black, she lay with her eyes open, overflowing with the thought of visiting the stars.

Her eyes closed, and she slept in fits and starts. She thought she might dream of distant lands, but she remembered nothing. The night crept along, achingly slowly. It was silly. The touch of the Investigator. She didn't even know her name. And she knew that they weren't hopping onto a jump-ship tomorrow. There wasn't even a plan. But it was coming. An hour before dawn, she fell into an uninterrupted sleep.

When she woke, the sun was up. She laughed to herself, stretching. When was the last time she had overslept? What a glorious morning it was.

She stayed in bed, sitting up and writing in her journal,

not bothering to change out of her night tunic. Her legs were under the blanket and she leaned back into the corner. At the sound of the knock at the door, she didn't bother looking up. "Come in!" she called. "I know, I'm late." She was finishing a sentence as she heard the door open and close. She raised her head and gasped.

The Principal stood in her room. This man had been bubbling with energy the day before. His joy and enthusiasm had been written all over his face and practically vibrated through his whole body. But that was a long day ago. Zeke did not understand how that shining person that she had last seen was the same person who stood before her.

His face was drawn and his eyes were red. His shoulders slumped. His eyes held nothing but pain.

"Principal?" Her voice held fear.

He stared at her, stricken and helpless. "Professor," he managed to say. "There's been an..." his voice trailed off. His eyes closed and his head shook back and forth. Zeke took a breath and set herself for the news. The Principal looked up to her again. "Professor Lin has gone," he said.

"Gone?" Zeke pulled back in surprise. "How? And where?"

The Principal awkwardly stepped forward and took her hands. He shook his head, once. "He's dead."

"That's not possible."

It was just ridiculous. Lin was a soldier who had fought for every major faction that humans had conjured up in his lifetime. His skin was knifeproof, bulletproof, and shock absorbent. His bones could rebuild themselves within a matter of seconds. He could breathe underwater. He could survive in the vacuum of space, for goodness sake. The Principal just looked at her.

"That's not possible."

Besides, he was working on a book. It was a children's

book where all the action was determined by whatever he dreamed. He would wake in the mornings and write down what he could remember from his dreams, and no matter how absurd it was, it went into the book. He joked that he had to keep a few things back to keep it appropriate. She told him to start a separate book for those dreams. Plus they were still in the middle of a chess game. And she was in bed, not even dressed properly. It wasn't possible. She shook her head.

"No."

"I found his body this morning," the Principal whispered. His eyes closed in pain.

"Where is he?" Fury began to rise in Zeke.

"The guest quarters," the Principal managed to say.

NINE

THE BODY

The Investigator stood over the body. The three officers stayed back, grim and silent. He was in his habit. His face was calm. There were no signs of damage.

"Tyrick," she said. He approached. "How long do we have?"

He sighed. "It's impossible to say exactly. Do you know when someone saw him last?"

"No," she said flatly.

Tyrick ducked his head. "Probably anywhere between twelve to twenty hours."

"And then he disintegrates?"

Tyrick nodded. "Nothing but ash at that point."

The Investigator frowned. "Help me," she said. Tyrick produced a knife and the two cut off Lin's habit. Tyrick cursed when he saw the skin. "Anything that could cause a fatal trauma? Check his head." They went over the body. "Anything?"

"No," said Tyrick, still staring at the scars. "Poison is the simplest explanation."

The Investigator looked at Tyrick. "Poison?" she repeated. "Poison did this?"

"He's a first generation soldier," said Tyrick. "It's unlikely. But it's possible and more likely than anything else."

"What are the other options?" Tyrick was silent. "Anyone?" she announced, looking back at Brighton and Third.

"Concentrated radiation?" asked Third.

Brighton shook his head. "There would be signs of

burning. What about..." he stopped. "That wouldn't work either."

The Investigator looked back at Tyrick. "Poison?" she asked, angrily.

He shrugged helplessly. "There were compounds developed to debilitate first-gen squads."

"Those gave people the shits!" the Investigator said.

Tyrick ducked his head again, staring at the floor. "It's possible they have been expanded on," he said quietly.

"Who the fuck would do that?" the Investigator demanded. "Who would spend time developing a weapon like that?" Tyrick was silent. "Who would waste time on that!" The room was very still. The Investigator snarled and turned to the window. It was a beautiful morning outside. The winds had relented and the sun was bright and not too warm.

The door burst open and the four turned. Zeke ran into the room and stopped, staring at Lin's naked body. Brighton stepped quickly to her and tried to turn her away. She brushed him aside and walked forward. Her face grew still as she looked down at the man in front of her. The Investigator watched the pain ripple in the professor's eyes.

She ran her head over his face. His eyes were closed and he looked very peaceful. But so cold. His touch had always been warm. No matter what the temperature was outside, no matter how harshly the wind cut around them as they walked. His hand was always warm.

"Is..." she started and swallowed. "Is that normal?" she asked.

"Is what normal?" asked Tyrick softly. She pointed to the scars that criss-crossed his body. Slightly elevated lines that circled him over and over. His legs, high on his arms. His torso. Sometimes one would run into another and stop. She hadn't known about this. He had kept them hidden all this time. "No, Professor," said Tyrick. "That's not normal at all."

"Where are his genitals?" she asked.

Tyrick looked surprised. "He's a soldier," he said simply.

"I don't know what that means."

"They're retracted," Tyrick said. "I thought you..." He paused. "And he..." He stopped again. "I'm sorry. I thought the two of you were intimate."

Zeke shook her head slowly. "Not like that," she said quietly. The Investigator lowered her eyes. Zeke reached out her hands and placed them on his chest. His chest that wasn't rising and falling. His chest that wasn't beating. His chest that was cold. His chest with scars that she had never seen. Never known about. Never known his pain.

She couldn't breathe. She stumbled backward, the Investigator catching her. The Principal stood in the doorway. She pulled away from the Investigator's arms, pushed past the Principal, went running down the hall. The corridors were empty as she fled back to her room, slamming the door. She stood in the space that was hers, her home. It felt like an alien world.

Zeke collapsed to her knees. Sitting there for a moment, she slowly turned and lay down flat on the ground. She stared at the ceiling, wondering where her tears were. Why wasn't she crying? Her eyes stayed open but darkness came over her.

The children sat in a circle, their arms entwined. Greta was crying the hardest. Their heads were bowed forward and her tears fell onto the stone floor. Each student wept. As their pain grew or they felt the pain of their neighbor, they tightened their grip, squeezed a little stronger. The small circle grew smaller as they compressed inward, pulling their friends close.

Geoffrey didn't understand. This wasn't supposed to happen. What did it even mean? How could Professor Lin not be there anymore? He held on tighter to Pency and Greta.

"Get a tissue sample," said the Investigator.

"With what?" said Tyrick. "I don't have a knife that can cut him."

"Get his stomach contents."

"With what! He's a walking tank. I can't open him up, I can't."

"Hold him upside down and shake him!" the Investigator shouted. "Figure it out!" Tyrick set his jaw forward and looked down. "Get the professors into the conference room," she snapped at Brighton and Third, who vanished quickly. "Do you have any ideas?" she said through clenched teeth.

He shook his head. "I can try to analyze the residuals once he breaks down."

"The ash!" The Investigator was incredulous. Tyrick let out an exasperated sigh and stared at her, challenging. The Investigator's eyes flashed and he looked back down. "Find out what you can," she said firmly, and walked out.

She stalked through the halls. This school had felt like it was cursed from the moment they arrived. It was a twisted spot. Even mining colonies had some kind of measurable change. They dug deeper into the ground or the ice or mire. Settlements expanded. Ships traveled. What was wrong with this place? One day was the same as the next and they all bled together.

Except this day. This day was different and all the ones that would come after it would be forever changed as well. This was the only thing that had happened to this damned school. The students and the teachers had been left here to be forgotten, to be forever in stasis. And now it was all in turmoil. Of course it would happen when she was here.

How could she have let this happen?

The Investigator stopped when she heard wailing. Her forehead creased as she identified the student quarters door. Cracking it open, she peered in. The students were huddled together, arms locked, a single mass, shuddering with the tears. She stared at the student body, unable to distinguish one from the next. Their grief was multiplied, and filled the room. She knew that one student had lost a mentor. She knew that they had all lost a pillar.

They had known nothing else. All their lives the professors here had been their guiding forces. And now one was ripped away. They had never known death before. How could they? The Investigator sighed to herself, and quietly closed the door. She continued down the hall, slower than before.

She reached the conference room and went in. Brighton and Third were there, standing against the wall by the door. The professors and the Principal were seated at the table, in silence. Three people were missing. One was back in the guest quarters, laying on a table. One was grieving.

"Where's bol Win?" she said. The faculty shook their heads. She turned to Brighton.

"I couldn't find him," he said.

Her face flinched in anger. "Find him anyway," she said. He nodded and vanished through the door.

"What have you brought to this school?" She turned to the table in surprise. Arden was glaring at her.

"Excuse me?"

"There's only one person here capable of killing a former soldier like Professor Lin," Arden said. His eyes turned to Third, who stood quietly. "Your hired dog there." Third kept his expression flat and his face pointed toward the ground.

"Please," the Principal pleaded. "We don't even know..." his voice trailed off in grief.

"Know what?" demanded Arden.

"We don't know how he died," said the Investigator. The group murmured. "Has anyone seen Professor bol Win?" she asked.

"Who cares?" exploded Arden. "You think the oldest man in the universe killed him?"

The Investigator shook with contained anger. "One man is dead and another missing and you don't care?" Arden slumped back slightly at the reproach.

"He's not..." the Principal started and stopped again, flustered. "I saw him early this morning, before..." he stopped again, his breath catching. "He was in the kitchen. He wasn't there later. I don't know where he is. I don't know." He held his head in his hands.

"What do you mean you don't know how he died?" asked Arden.

The Investigator looked annoyed. "I mean we don't know how he died." Arden leaned back in his chair and a strange look passed over his face. "What is it?" asked the Investigator.

He was silent for a moment, staring down at the table. "Professor bol Win," he said.

"You think he was involved?"

Arden shook his head. "No, that's not what I mean. He's..." he sighed. "He's deteriorating."

The table murmured again, louder. "I don't know how we can say that," said the Principal.

"You examined him," said Arden. "With the other officer."

"We didn't find anything."

"What if you missed it?" accused Arden. "What if the treatment is breaking down? What if this is just the beginning? What if it starts to happen to all of us?"

The Investigator watched the argument play out. Fear and paranoia and confusion. She turned to Third. "This isn't helping us. Keep an eye on them." Third nodded.

"What are you saying?" demanded Arden. The

Investigator turned. All those at the table had turned to face them now. Alone among them, the Principal looked sad. The others looked fearful and angry. "What if you brought an infection?" The Investigator closed her eyes, exasperated. "Are we prisoners here now? Is that what he's here for?" She walked out of the room with the accusations following her.

Stalking back down the hall, the Investigator saw the student quarters door was open and the crying had stopped. She looked in again.

The students still sat in a circle but now Zeke was in the middle, sitting on her knees, her hands in her lap. Her face was wet and her eyes sparkled with tears. She was talking quietly and the students stared up at her. They asked questions and she answered. Greta scooted forward, dropping her head in Zeke's lap and Zeke gently laid her hand on the child's head and continued to answer their questions. They asked about death. They asked about Lin. They asked what he had liked. They asked what he had done before he came here. They asked where he was now.

Zeke spoke softly with her voice full of care. Her answers were clear and honest. She spoke quietly and the Investigator was too far to hear everything but she was mesmerized by the calm presence that Zeke created. She stared at the professor, spellbound.

Standing in the doorway, Zeke noticed her at last. Surrounded by her wards, she looked directly at the Investigator. Pain and strength were etched across her face. The children noticed and turned as well. The Investigator stood in the path of their gaze. They didn't speak, their faces were blank.

The Investigator nodded once and turned away.

The four were back in the guest quarters. Lin's body lay uncovered in front of them. The Investigator's jaw was clenched. She bit back question after question that she already knew the answer to. Did Brighton find bol Win? Of course he didn't. Did Tyrick know what killed Lin? Of course he didn't. Was Third ready to fight? Of course he was.

Finally the Investigator spoke. "If he's alive, he's the suspect. If he's dead, then we know something else. Is he going to disintegrate if he's dead?"

"No," said Tyrick. "That's just soldiers."

"If he's in the sea we won't find him. If he crests the ridge, the proximity sensor will alert?" She looked at Brighton, who nodded. "You and Third will continue to search the rocks." She turned to Tyrick. "You'll analyze the remains once he..." she stopped and shook her head.

Someone knocked at the door. The Principal gently opened it and looked in. "May I?" he said. The Investigator nodded and he crept into the room, his face drawing in pain as he looked at Lin. He approached the body and put his hand over his mouth. "Oh," he said softly. "Was this my fault?" He stared up at the Investigator. "Did you bring an infection?" he asked fearfully.

"That's not..." the Investigator stopped. "We have no reason to think that," she said. "We're doing everything we can right now and I will find out what happened here," she said firmly.

The Principal ran his hand over his face. He looked weary. "Will we be able to have a..." he struggled. "A ceremony? For the body," his voice caught. "For Professor Lin."

The Investigator looked at Tyrick without turning her head. He frowned. "We still need to examine the body," she said quietly.

"After, I mean," said the Principal.

The Investigator closed her eyes. "There won't be a body after," she said.

"What?"

Tyrick cleared his throat. "Soldiers were designed so that their cells would deteriorate rapidly following their death. It was intended to..." he sighed. "To avoid large collections of..." he trailed off. "Following a battle," he said.

The Principal looked confused. "Avoid rotting bodies?" he said. Tyrick nodded. "Oh," the Principal said. He turned to look at Lin again. "Can we say our goodbyes here at least?" he said. He turned to the Investigator. "Please," he said quietly.

"Chief?" Tyrick said, leaning his head to the side. The Investigator walked to the window at the end of the room and he followed. The Principal waited by Lin. "It's possible there's a window once he starts to break down. I may be able to collect tissue samples while they're weakened and run tests before they disintegrate."

The Investigator thought for a moment. "Do you know when the process will start?"

Tyrick wagged his head back and forth. "I don't know. His skin is getting a little more..." he shrugged. "Soft? I think I should be able to cut into it at some point. But I don't know how long this whole breakdown takes."

"Alright," said the Investigator. "It's your call. Can they see the body beforehand?"

"It has to be quick." The Investigator nodded.

They came in single-file, students interspersed with faculty. One by one they came to the table where Lin lay covered. They stopped and stood for a moment. Their faces were confused. What had they been expecting? What kind of feeling of closure might this have brought? There was nothing. There was nothing they could do. There were no answers for them here. Just a sheet on a table, outlining a shape that they no longer knew. Their friend and teacher had left this place and would never return, not even for all the time they had.

Zeke came last. She didn't approach the table but looked at the Investigator instead. The Investigator couldn't meet her gaze.

Tyrick caught the Principal. "Where's the boy?" he asked.

"Hm?"

"Geoffrey."

"Oh," the Principal said, looking around. "I don't know."

TEN
THE BOOKS

He stumbled over the rocks, his habit catching on the edges, his sandals slipping. He didn't want to see Professor Lin. He didn't want any of this to have happened. He wanted to go back to classes. He wanted everything to be normal. He crossed the outer path and kept moving toward the distant ridge. The boulder field lay in front of him.

"It's the habits," said Third. "We could walk within five meters of him and not see anything." Brighton didn't say anything. He stared at an aerial image of the school and surrounding area. "Are you listening to me? We need a sweep line. With everybody, it wouldn't take too long."

"You want the kids to stumble across a body?" said Brighton, still looking at the map.

Third shrugged. "I don't know. I don't know anything about kids," he muttered.

"We're going to run in a zig-zag sweep," Brighton said, pointing. "You'll go here and bounce back and forth from the school to the ridge line."

"What kind of angles?"

Brighton sighed. "As close to thirty as you can manage but..." he trailed off. "You're right about the sweep. This is a stab in the dark if he's not moving. He's either dead or doesn't want to be found so we're just hoping to get lucky until we can organize a group. After the..." he paused. "Funeral." He held up the map again. "We'll probably connect around here."

"That's not fair," said Third.

"You shouldn't be so fast," said Brighton.

Geoffrey fell forward, scuffing his shin on a rock. He winced and sat down, holding it tight. Blood seeped through his habit, mixing with the red dust that already stained it. The pain radiated and intensified. Tears streamed down his face. It hurt so much.

Sitting alone among the rocks, Geoffrey began to sob. He beat his hands against the ground and stomped his feet. His cries wafted into the wind and were lost. He was just a small boy and no one could hear him and no one cared about him and his shin hurt and he was sorry any of this had ever happened.

He stopped crying and sat in the dust, sniffling. His face was streaked with tears and dust and his habit was a mess. Pulling up the hem, he looked at his leg. There was an ugly gash and it was turning into a welt already.

"That looks like it hurts."

Geoffrey jumped backward, falling over another rock. He scrambled in reverse on his hands until a large boulder stopped him. Professor bol Win hadn't moved.

"And what brings you out this way, young Geoffrey?" asked Professor bol Win. Now he took a step forward. Geoffrey instinctively pressed back into the rock behind him. "Out for a stroll?" Another step. "Getting away from it all?" Another. He was just a meter or two away from the boy. "Or..." he leaned down, leering into Geoffrey's face. "Looking for something?"

"I..." Geoffrey stammered, confused and afraid.

"There, there," said Professor bol Win. He stepped back now and went and sat down on a rock. "Let us have a chat, you and I," he said. Geoffrey stared at him, petrified, but not knowing why. "You children," Professor bol Win laughed. "You think you have the run of the school. You think you know everything that happens while your poor teachers are just left in the dark. You and your little games," he finished softly. "Well," he laughed again. "You do know something I don't, don't you?" Geoffrey stared in confusion. "The story. The book. How did you do it?"

"I..." Geoffrey stammered again, trailing off.

"Enough!" Professor bol Win shouted, standing and towering over Geoffrey. "Enough with the delays! Enough with the lies and the half-truths! Enough spinning this charade along!" He reached down and grabbed Geoffrey's habit, pulling him up. "Tell me!"

"I don't know!" Geoffrey cried.

Professor bol Win shook him. "Tell me!"

"I don't know!" he shrieked.

"Where are the other books?" Professor bol Win shouted.

"What?" Geoffrey sputtered.

Professor bol Win violently threw him to the ground and he shouted in pain. Before Geoffrey could respond, the teacher had him around the wrist and was pulling or dragging him over the ground. Geoffrey tried to get up, tried to navigate over the rocks that cut and scraped him. Stumbling along, he was just as suddenly thrown to the ground again. They were behind a massive boulder, the school completely hidden from view. There was a small pile of rocks off to one side and a strange pit in the ground. Inside was a chest, closed. It looked like it had once been red but had faded with severe wear.

"Where are the others?" Profesor bol Win shouted again. Geoffrey rolled onto his side in agony, trying to hold onto his arms and legs all at the same time. "The others!" the professor shouted. He knelt down over the chest and opened it. He reached inside and started throwing out the contents. A book sailed past Geoffrey's head, followed by another.

Despite the shooting pains in his limbs, Geoffrey gaped at

the pages fluttering around him. Books. Books he had never seen. Books he had only heard of. Books he had never heard of. The Peregrines. Don Quixote. A Sound of Waves. He picked one up out of the dust. Professor bol Win was still reaching into the chest and shouting.

"It isn't here! Where are the others?" He reached the bottom of the chest. Grabbing the last book he whirled around, raising it high. The boy was gone.

The wind had picked up and was starting to swirl around him. Professor bol Win stood by the boulder, his arm still raised dumbly over his head, clutching the book he had intended to hurl at a child. He stared at the scattered books, pages flapping in the wind, surrounding him. So much time. So much time. How long? How long had each writer pored over their work, shaping it and bending the words to their will? And how long had it taken to copy each one of these out? How long had they lay here? What were the odds that words written countless ages ago would end up littering the feet of this broken professor on a shattered land?

Professor bol Win started to laugh. It was too much. It was too obvious. They didn't believe him, of course. They couldn't see. It was simple enough to demonstrate though, even in a way that their minds could grasp. He started walking.

Tyrick hissed as the proximity sensor alerted. The Investigator looked up. Tyrick was bent over Lin's body. "Someone's at the path up the ridge," said Tyrick.

"What's the status here?"

Tyrick cursed. "I need..." he started.

"Stick with it," the Investigator said, and was out the door.

She raced through the halls, bursting outside, and leaning into a full sprint toward the ridge. Dust flew up behind her as her feet landed perfectly among the jumbled rocks. She was making a beeline toward the path they had come down when they first arrived. It seemed like such a very long time ago. As she ran, she opened her mouth and emitted a short, sharp shriek into the air.

Third was close enough to catch it. He clambered onto a boulder and looked out across the wasteland. There was the Investigator, running like a person possessed. She was heading straight for the ridge. The sensor must have tripped. Third jumped down and took off for the ridge.

Geoffrey came stumbling back into the courtyard. The children were huddled there with Professor Zeke, looking out across the rocks. The Investigator had torn past them and they couldn't help but follow.

"Geoffrey!" Pency shouted. He ran to his friend, who collapsed, covered in sweat and blood and grime. The other children and Professor Zeke quickly followed. Professor Zeke took charge instantly.

"Get a kit from inside," she said firmly to Greta, who turned and ran. "Bring water," she said to Stephen, who turned and ran. "Bring the Principal," she said to Wint, who turned and ran.

Pency held onto Geoffrey's hand as he lay in Zeke's lap, shivering. "What's wrong with him?" he asked, terrified.

"He's in a bit of shock," said Professor Zeke, softly. "Back up, children," she said. They all did, except for Pency.

Geoffrey turned up to face Professor Zeke. "It's Professor bol Win," he whispered. "He did it."

"What did he do, Geoffrey?" asked Professor Zeke.

"I don't know," Geoffrey cried, burying his head back into Professor Zeke's shoulder.

The Investigator was racing up the switchbacks on the ridge when Third reached the base. He leapt at the steep grade, clawing his way straight up with great speed, ignoring the winding path. The Investigator continued to sprint on the path, seeing Third bounding up below her. She reached the summit just before him. He had a wild look in his eyes.

"The sensor tripped," she gasped. He nodded, without speaking, taking deep gulps of air. They looked across the flat expanse, and quickly saw the cause of their race.

Professor bol Win was slowly standing up. He was a distance aways, and walked casually toward the edge of the cliff. The drop below him was sheer and about three hundred meters to the ground. Third groaned and shook his head, as if to clear it. The Investigator took a deep breath and started walking toward the professor.

"Hello there," bol Win called out.

"Hello," replied the Investigator. Third had started following her, hands on his hips, disinterested and annoyed.

"Have you figured it out yet?" bol Win called.

"Not yet," said the Investigator. "Why don't you explain it for me?"

Bol Win laughed mirthlessly. "You wouldn't understand. I tried, remember?"

"Oh, yes," grumbled Third.

"Have you ever been caught in a rainstorm?" bol Win shouted.

"A rain storm?" The Investigator sighed. After just a relatively short amount of time around the Principal, she had begun to appreciate his intense dislike for leading questions. Bol Win waited and she shook her head. "Yes," she called to him, exasperated.

"Did you get wet?"

"I ran for this?" Third muttered.

"Yes," the Investigator said, approaching closer.

"What are the odds, do you suppose, of that?" bol Win said, smirking.

The Investigator sighed again. "The odds of what?"

"Getting wet."

"Pretty good," said the Investigator, growing more and more annoyed.

"Want me to grab him?" asked Third.

"Ah, ah!" bol Win admonished. He stepped closer to the edge. "I don't have your gifts," he said. "This is fatal." Third stared at him, confused. "So, pretty good?" bol Win turned back to the Investigator.

"Pretty good," the Investigator repeated.

"But look at the odds for a single raindrop hitting you," bol Win said. "A single raindrop and a single person. Millions of droplets falling, you occupy a tiny space in the storm, a moving target no less. Trying to find cover, but high above you a droplet forms and begins to fall, getting tossed this way and that by the wind. As you run, and as it falls, the two are drawn toward each other like magnets. Until," he clapped his heads together. "The most unlikely event happens. It strikes you square in head."

"Alright," said the Investigator.

"Statistically impossible, one might say," bol Win said. "But what are the odds of escaping a rain storm without getting wet?" He stared at the Investigator. "Statistically impossible, one might say. Eventually, no matter how unusual the event is, the most unlikely things will happen. It just takes enough repetition. Enough time." He took another step toward the edge. The Investigator mirrored the step and he held up a hand, stopping her. "And time is something we have an abundance of, for one perfectly acceptable reason."

"What reason?" the Investigator asked.

Bol Win laughed. "I already told you," he said.

"I'm tired of this," the Investigator said.

"Do you require more proof?" bol Win asked.

The Investigator narrowed her eyes. "Is that what Professor Lin was? Proof? He's still dead."

"We're all dead!" bol Win cackled. Stepping backward

once more he disappeared from view. Third grunted in surprise and dashed to the edge, jumping off.

"What on the world?" the Investigator said to herself. She looked around, standing by herself at the edge of the world. The school lay far below her and all around stretched a seemingly endless scrub waste. The air was calm. It seemed impossible that a moment ago she had been having a conversation and now here she was alone. She thought about trying to look over the edge and decided against it. Sighing once more, she turned and started to make her way back down the path.

By the time she reached the body, Brighton was there. He had seen the professor fall and Third follow. Third was lounging on a rock. Professor bol Win was a broken mess. Brighton was crouched over the body and he shook his head at the Investigator as she approached. She looked at Third.

"Any last words that I missed?"

He shook his head. "It would have been instant."

She stared up at the ridge, three hundred meters above them, then back down to Third. "Hurt yourself?" He shook his head again.

"Can we go home now?" asked Brighton.

ELEVEN

The Debriefing

The Investigator stared out of the window in the faculty conference room. It was growing dark outside and the shadows were lengthening, making the rocks seem alien and more distant. Their time here was drawing to a close and she felt strange. Relief mixed with regret. She and her team had traveled great distances and seen many unusual things but this place and its unsettling calm made her uncomfortable. Behind her, the Principal, Arden, Zeke, Nalin, and Tyrick sat around the long table.

Brighton and Third trudged in loudly, Third banging his knee on the door. They were carrying a chest that looked like it had once been red.

"Is that it?" asked Arden.

The Investigator turned a sideways glance to the Principal and caught him wince. He saw her notice and smiled softly. What a ridiculous and pointless question.

The two officers dropped the chest on the table and Arden and Nalin both stood up for it. Arden opened the top and began rifling through the contents, letting out a deep exhalation. "This is..." He turned over another book. "Quite the collection." Nalin was inspecting the lining of the chest.

Zeke didn't move. The Principal eyed the chest disinterestedly. As Arden began stacking books on the table the Principal absentmindedly took one and began flipping through it. He set it back down after a few moments. "So what happened?" he said, sighing.

The Investigator turned back to look out the window. Tyrick stared at her, expectantly, but she remained silent.

"Well," said Tyrick, hesitantly. "Professor Lin was poisoned." He stopped, waiting. When nothing happened, he continued. "It appears..." He paused again, looking again at the Investigator, who remained quiet. "It appears that Professor bol Win was keeping a hidden collection of books outside. Lin probably found about it somehow and bol Win killed him to keep it quiet. Geoffrey must have seen Carmilla in the collection at some point. Memorized it and copied it. Or maybe read it and retained it somehow," he finished, lamely. Again he looked in vain to the Investigator's back. She remained motionless.

"But Carmilla isn't here," said Arden.

"He may have had more than one collection," said Tyrick. "There could be other caches out there." He jerked his head to the window. "Can you tell who copied the books?" Arden picked one up and stared intently at one of the pages. "I don't suppose it would be on the cover page," said Tyrick.

The Principal chuckled softly, sadly. "No," he said. He glanced at the closest book to him. "And my eyes can't tell the difference between the professors' handwriting. But Arden is the expert."

Arden frowned. "I can't say for certain, but..." he pointed to the page. "The indentations here do..." he paused again. "Yes, the lowercase gee here." He turned the book to the Principal, who looked at it briefly, then shrugged. "I would say it's Professor bol Win's handwriting," Arden said. "Professor Nalin could do analysis on it."

"What's the point?" sighed the Principal.

"What are we going to do about Geoffrey?" asked Zeke, softly. She looked at the Principal who turned his face to the table, miserable. "We don't have any proof he copied anything." The room was silent as she stared at the Principal, who didn't respond. "We can't..."

"What else is there?" the Principal snapped, interrupting.

Zeke sat back, startled. The Principal glowered in his seat. "What other option is there? The boy cheated." He frowned deeper. "He plagiarized and now two professors are dead."

"He didn't have anything to do with it!" Zeke said. "He was trying to figure it out, just like the rest of us. That whole mess with the note."

"Hm?" said Arden.

"The note they put under bol Win's door. Geoffrey wrote it. He was trying his best!" she pleaded to the Principal. Arden stared blankly. "We have to do right by him." The Principal stared at the ground. "Please," she said. "We have to..."

"I don't!" the Principal stopped abruptly. "I don't," he said again, softer. "We can't." He closed his eyes and covered his face with his hands.

"What about our tour?" asked Zeke, her voice breaking. "What about our journey?" Tears welled up in her eyes. The Principal shook his head. "We were going to spread our work. To, to spark," she stopped. It was all falling apart.

"We'll just..." the Principal said softly. "We'll just go back to the way things were. We'll just go back to normal." Zeke slumped in her chair. "It's too dangerous," the Principal said. "I need to keep them safe. I need to keep them safe," he repeated.

The room was very still and very quiet. The Investigator watched the shadows outside, wishing that things were just a little bit different. It had been so close.

"I..." Arden broke the silence. "I'm sorry. We can't go back to normal," he said. Zeke looked up at him, hopefully. The Principal turned to him as well. "The boy," said Arden, avoiding Zeke's eyes. "He has to be expelled."

"What?" Zeke exploded out of her chair. Arden stepped backward quickly.

"He can't stay here," he said, raising his hands.

"Then I'm going with him!"

"You can't," Arden said softly. "He has to go back to Central Authority."

"Central?" Zeke spluttered. "Since when?"

"He has to be placed with a family," Arden said.

"I'll take him!"

"You're not..." Arden sighed. "You're not qualified," he finished.

"Qualified?" Zeke gasped. Tears fell down her face. "I have looked after that boy," she stopped, as a sob shook her. "For ages." She stared at Arden. "I can."

"Can what?" Arden interrupted. "You wouldn't have a job. You wouldn't have a home. Your only skill has been instructing children and there's not much of a market for that out there, is there? He needs a family who can take care of him." He sat down abruptly. Zeke stared at him with wide eyes, then turned and strode out the door.

Arden turned to the Principal. "I can take him to the outer jump pad. We can leave in the morning." The Principal said nothing and didn't look up. Arden nodded once to himself, then stood and walked out. Nalin followed suit.

Tyrick jerked his head at the other two officers and they started to leave. The Investigator caught Tyrick's eye and nodded at the departing Nalin. Tyrick blinked in acknowledgment.

In the hallway, Tyrick touched Nalin's elbow. "Excuse me, Professor Nalin. Why didn't our initial scan detect the books hidden in the rocks?"

"The chest was lined with something," Nalin said. "It's not a mask exactly, but it distorts the chemical signature that the books excrete. Changes it."

"Can you search for this new signature?"

"With the proper equipment."

He pulled out a tablet. "Access Persephone ground scanner. Lock other functions. New temporary user." He handed it to Nalin. "You can use this."

"Persephone?"

"Our ship."

Back in the conference room, it was quiet again. The Investigator stood and the Principal sat and they stayed in silence while the light faded. The Principal finally stirred, noticing the gloom. "Light, please," he sighed. The room illuminated. "Ach," he muttered. "Sixty percent." The room dimmed.

The Investigator finally turned around and came to sit down across from the Principal. She collapsed into the chair, and the two regarded each other. "I'm sorry about your friends," said the Investigator. The Principal shut his eyes in pain.

"How am I even supposed to feel?" he said. "How do I feel about bol Win?" He opened his eyes again, looking at the Investigator, pleading.

She felt helpless. "How do you feel?" she asked, emphasizing the second word.

He gestured hopelessly. "Sad. Angry. Betrayed. Sad." He stared down at the table and put his hands in his lap. "I'm so sad," he whispered. "He was my friend. Lin was my friend. Why are they gone?" He looked up again at the Investigator. "Why?"

"Sometimes there are no answers," the Investigator said. "Sometimes we just have to live with..." She struggled. "With the uncertainty." The Principal sighed and closed his eyes again. They were both silent again. The Investigator broke the quiet. "I've done nothing here," she said.

The Principal opened his eyes in surprise. "What do you mean?" he said.

She looked at him. "What have I done? Asked some questions. Looked around. Endlessly, it felt like. What did I do? What did I solve?"

"Well, you..." the Principal started and stopped. "You..." he stopped again. "No, you didn't do anything, did you?" The two laughed, softly, sadly. The Principal stopped and covered his face with his hands. His shoulders shook briefly. His eyes were red when he took his hands away and he sniffled. He shook his head, to clear it. "Not quite one of Dupin's cases, is it?" he said softly.

"Who?" The Investigator looked at him.

"Monsieur Dupin," the Principal said, with an exaggerated accent the Investigator couldn't place. "He was the first detective. In fiction," he added. "Edger Allen Poe?" He looked questioningly at the Investigator, who shook her head. "Poe was the author. The Raven?" Another shake of the head. "Mm. You know," he gave a small, embarrassed laugh. "I thought when you first arrived that this would be like one of those stories. A detective story. Sherlock Holmes."

"I know that one," said the Investigator.

The Principal smiled. "Silly, isn't it? To expect this life to mimic one that was not only fictional, but also one from before, my goodness..." He stopped and a haunted look crossed over his face. "From before space travel. How long?" He looked to the Investigator. "How long has it been? How long have I been here? How long have I been alive?"

"I don't know," the Investigator said. "It's impossible to say."

"How many cycles?" the Principal asked, sitting forward, suddenly urgent.

"I, I don't know," the Investigator said. The Principal slumped backward. "It's been," she shrugged. "Hundreds."

"Hundreds," the Principal breathed. "Hundreds of cycles. Hundreds of hundreds. Tens of thousands." He was staring into the middle distance. "Do you know," he said, still staring into nothing. "Before the treatment, you were lucky to reach sixty years. Sixty orbits. Can you imagine that," he said, flatly.

"Sixty. And now this. I've lived longer than all of the recorded history that existed when I was born."

The Investigator stared at him in silence for a moment. "Why are you abandoning your plan?" she asked.

His gaze fel, and he stared at his hands in his lap. He rubbed them together. He frowned. "I just can't," he said.

"What about being afraid of the same old patterns?"

He winced. "I'm sorry," he said. "But it's too much. It's too much." He looked up at her. "It's stopped me."

"It doesn't have to," she said, leaning forward.

The Principal shook his head. "Now? With a plagiarism case? How would anyone listen to us, even if..." he trailed off. "Even if we had the strength." The Investigator sighed. "I'm sorry," the Principal said again. "But it will go back to the way it was. We'll hire a new professor. And continue on our path." The Investigator shifted, uncomfortable. The Principal noticed. "What?"

She sat there, miserable. "That may not be possible," she said, softly.

"What on the world do you mean?"

"Central Authority," she said, still softly, still with pain. "They may..." she trailed off.

"May what?" the Principal demanded.

There wasn't a way around this any longer. "They may shut the school down," she said. The Principal jerked backward as if he had been struck.

"Shut the school down?" he gasped.

The Investigator dropped her head to her hands. "You don't know what it's like out there anymore. You don't know what..." she stopped and looked up to him. "Coming here, it was like coming back in time," she said. "This place, it'..." she shrugged. "It's an island. You must know that, don't you?"

The Principal's face was nothing but confusion. He blankly shook his head.

"You, you write books," said the Investigator. "You write books for people who don't read. Many can't anymore. Did you know that?" He shook his head again, slowly. "It doesn't matter to them. This place, this school. They've..." She stopped, knowing she couldn't absolve herself. "We've..." she emphasized. "Moved on."

"Moved on?" the Principal still was in a state of shock. "To what?"

The Investigator shook her head. "I don't even know," she said quietly. "It feels like we're just in a sort of stasis now. Comfortable and complacent. Isn't that what civilization was supposed to bring? Shouldn't we be happy with that?"

"Are you?" the Principal asked. "Are you happy?"

"Some are."

"Are you?" the Principal asked again, pointedly.

The Investigator met his stare. "No," she said.

"Then we write books for you," the Principal said. "And people like you. There must be others."

The Investigator looked helpless. "Even I don't read books anymore," she said. "It's just not something that's done."

"Well you can start!" the Principal said, louder than he had expected. He started to feel a panic rising in him. "What are you even doing here?"

"What?"

"What are you doing here?" he was almost shouting. "If Central doesn't care, why would they care about this school, why would they send an investigator for a case of plagiarism?" The Investigator looked down at her lap. "Why did they send you?" he demanded.

She said nothing. The silence hung heavy in the room.

"They didn't send you to investigate a case of plagiarism," the Principal said flatly.

"No," the Investigator said, softly. "I was not sent for that reason. It was just an excuse. To evaluate the school."

The Principal leaned back in his chair, slowly. "Evaluate?" he whispered. "Why not send..." He waved his hands out. "An evaluator!"

"There's no such thing. There's no one there anymore who was around when the schools were founded," she said. "People have transferred or quit."

"What about..." the Principal paused, trying to recall names. Nothing came to him.

"They received your report about the plagiarism and decided to use it as an excuse to evaluate the school to determine if it should be shut down. And if the other programs should be halted as well. And my team and I were the closest."

The Principal laughed softly. "All this time you were here," he said.

"My report..." the Investigator said. "I will recommend this school stay open, but..." She paused. "There won't be any new professors." The Principal nodded, as if to himself. "And I can't promise they won't shut the school down anyway."

Throughout the night, the students and faculty and guests slept fitfully. None of them expected to sleep at all, but they were all exhausted. It was a restless and painful night. Covers tangled and it was impossible to get comfortable. Greta and Stephen had lost their mentors. They barely grasped the loss, but it was more than the other students. The faculty had lost friends and had to contend with the idea that one had murdered another. No one felt more pain than Zeke. It overwhelmed her quickly though and she fell into a sleep deeper than the rest but still shot through with unpleasant dreams.

In the middle of the night, she woke. There was no solace here for her. And there wouldn't be again. She got up in her shift and walked out of her room. Wandering the halls in the dark, she cried softly. Through the halls that she knew she couldn't come back to. The Principal would probably tell her to give it some time. But there wasn't enough time.

Turning a corner, she was startled to see a light on in the kitchen and hear someone cluttering. Tyrick was cutting a slice of bread. When he turned, she was standing in the doorway, like a spirit.

"Fuck me," he gasped, still gripping the knife.

"I'm sorry," Zeke said, blankly.

"You startled me." Zeke nodded, still with a vacant expression. "Sorry," he said. "I wanted to get some of this bread while I still can." He looked around. "Is the butter around?" Zeke walked in, opening a cupboard and taking out the butter. "Thanks. Want one?" he asked, pointing the knife at the bread.

"No," she said, taking a cup from a shelf. She got herself water and leaned back against the wall.

Tyrick busied himself with the bread and butter. He felt uncomfortable. He didn't know what to say. Zeke was quiet. He finished with the bread and took a bite.

"Where will you go next?" asked Zeke.

"Hm? Um, home," Tyrick said around the bread. "We're, the officers, are stationed out of Musken. The Investigator doesn't have a set assignment."

"Do you have a family?"

Tyrick swallowed. "Yes, of a sorts. Adopted," he smiled. She looked at him quizzically. "You could say I was adopted," he said. "After the wars, there were a lot of lost soldiers." She nodded to herself. "I was taken in and found a home. It's..." He thought about it. The trees and the water. "A special place for me." She nodded again, taking a drink of water. "Your man..." said Tyrick. Zeke looked up sharply.

"He wasn't my man," she said, softly.

Tyrick glanced at her. "Your friend. You saw his body?"

She nodded. "You saw the scars?" She nodded again. "Do you know..." He paused, weighing the balance between being delicate and being honest. "Do you know what kind of energy transfer is required to cause damage to someone like Lin?" She shook her head. "It's..." He shrugged, staring into a corner. "Immense." He looked to Zeke. "That man experienced the kind of trauma that I can't even have nightmares about. I don't know how he was still standing at the end of it all." Zeke stared at him. "And not just the physical pain. He was reprogrammed eight times?" She didn't respond. "That's..." He waved the bread in the air. "I've never heard of that. You remember everything, you know?" She shook her head gently. "Being reprogrammed. Your memories don't get wiped. It's as if one day you like strawberries and the next day you don't. One day you're fighting for the Eurasion Bloc and the next what you want is to be a pirate bouncing freighters off of Mars." Zeke creased her brow in confusion at the terms. "But you still remember you liked strawberries. You remember their taste. They make you repulsed now, but you remember eating them." He shook his head as if to clear it. "It spins you around. Eight. I can't imagine." Tyrick shook his head again, slower, taking another bite. "He had a horrific time," he said quietly. Zeke hung her head and closed her eyes.

For a few moments, the only sound was Tyrick crunching on the bread crust. Then Zeke spoke, softly. "Long ago," she said. "Soldiers from a defeated army were conscripted into the army that had defeated them. I always imagined reprogramming was like that. One day you're fighting for someone and the next for someone else. It doesn't matter, because the fight doesn't matter. It's just brutal, pointless violence." Resentment and anger filled her words.

"Hm," Tyrick grunted. "That's a good way of looking at it. I figured reprogramming was just a cheap way to acquire a soldier." He took another bite. "But you're right," he said, around the bread. "Pointless." He shook his head.

"What was it like?" Zeke asked, staring blankly into the middle distance.

"What was what like?"

"Going from war to peace."

"Did you ever ask Lin that?"

"No," said Zeke, still staring into a space that Tyrick couldn't see.

Tyrick took a deep breath and exhaled. First Third and now Zeke. "I was in combat at the time. I mean, the exact moment the broadcast went out."

"Oh?" Now she finally blinked, and looked up at him.

"Mm," he murmured. "Getting shot at. I remember I was crouching behind a wall while puffs of dirt kept bouncing up into my eyes from the bullet rounds hitting the ground in front of me."

"Projectiles?"

He nodded. "I remember thinking how," he shrugged. "Insane, just insane, all of it was." He took another bite. He was definitely going to miss the bread. "How pointless. And then the broadcast came onto our HUDs." Zeke looked confused. "The information display in our helmets." She nodded. "I remember the bullets stopped hitting around me. I remember looking at my squad and seeing the same surprise in all of their eyes." He closed his eyes, sending himself back into that moment, covered in sweat and grime and body armor, clutching a rifle. "Everyone just sort of stood up and we all stared at each other. You know, I can't even remember who we were fighting. But I remember staring across this street at a soldier who had just been trying to kill me. He was holding the rifle in his hand, looking down at it, like he couldn't believe how it had got there. I don't know," he shrugged again. "It was as if everyone in that street realized all at the exact same moment how pointless it had been that we were trying to annihilate each other. How important could the reason have been if it could be stopped by a single order?" He gave a small laugh and took another bite of the diminishing piece of bread.

"Was it like being reprogrammed?" she asked.

"A bit, I suppose." He scoffed. "Certainly more pleasant."

"What's the actual process like? Reprogramming."

Tyrick winced. "Reprogramming is..." He hesitated. "...was... a very involved, very painful procedure." He shook his head. "Eight times," he muttered. Zeke closed her eyes at the thought. "Hey," Tyrick said. She looked up again. "How long was he here? Lin."

Zeke shrugged. "A long time," she said.

"I don't know much more about the man than I could hear about from his file and the few times we spoke," Tyrick said. "But I know one thing. This place," he gestured around at the room. "This place was the best thing that ever happened to him. Trust me. What he found here was peace and there was no one more deserving. And you helped bring him that peace. He had a good life here." Tears fell from Zeke's eyes. "He had a good life here," Tyrick repeated. "It's not about the amount of time." He frowned. "I don't know everything that you're going through. I can't say how you should feel or that things will get better. But I'll just ask you to do one thing." Zeke looked up to him. "When you remember him, along with everything else, remember that he found joy here. Joy and peace. And that's such a rare thing. He was very lucky."

She found the Investigator standing uncomfortably outside her room. The Investigator looked startled and guilty when she had come around the corner, the way the children did sometimes when they were found out for shirking on chores. But the Investigator recovered her composure as she approached, her face shifting into a look of concern and compassion, but also with a question behind it, a question that the Investigator knew she shouldn't be asking. Not now.

Neither spoke. Zeke hesitated at her door, considering the two options. She could go in and close the door softly behind her and stay in the dark. Sleep would probably not find her, and she would sit in her mind, questions spinning, fragments of memories surfacing, each one so frustratingly incomplete or inaccurate. She could grieve. Or she could take the Investigator by the hand and lead her in. For a time anyway, she could be distracted from all of it. She could set aside the questions, set aside the grief, set aside her pain for a moment, knowing that she would take it back again. She took the Investigator's hand.

Later, as they lay together, she felt the tears start. With her eyes closed, she felt the Investigator's gentle hand brush each one away. She thought she would sob but nothing came except for more tears, each one falling faster than the last, each one picked up by the fingertips of the person who watched over her.

"Thank you," she whispered.

She opened blurry eyes and the tears came cascading down. Now finally a sob took her, followed by another. The Investigator cradled her as she wept.

There was nothing but darkness that she thought would last forever. Nothing seemed to be real, no sensation, no thought. It was the end of it all, at long last, the end of the universe, the end of life. But the window began to turn gray, as it always did, as it always would while she lived in this room. Against every conceivable thought, the world continued to turn, with total disregard for her.

It would keep turning, on and on, until the sun devoured it. The universe would keep expanding until it started to collapse, falling back in on itself until it reached a single point where it would explode again, generating new stars, new planets, new life, new consciousnesses, new loves, until they all withered and died. Would she be among them again? Would she meet Lin once more? Would she be held by the Investigator? What possible chance of that could there be?

"Your officer," she said. The Investigator's eyes snapped open, confused for a moment, before focusing in on her. "Third. He is of the protector class, is he not?"

"He is," the Investigator said.

"What a life that would be. Have any of them been killed yet?"

"No, not yet. Not through lack of trials."

"Oh? I thought they were bred after major combat operations had ceased."

"They were, but they're often used for exploration of the most extreme planetary environments. Diamond rain falling sideways at supersonic speeds. Oceans of lava, poison gas, cold that breaks rock. And we never know if we're going to encounter a hostile sentience."

Zeke scoffed quietly then was silent for a moment. "Is it true that they were originally created to defend against the androids?"

The Investigator shifted. She had been laying on her side, fully stretched out. Now she straightened and sat up slightly, wishing for an extra pillow as she leaned her head back against the wall. "That depends on who you ask," she said. The bed was small and she moved her arm around Zeke, mostly because it had nowhere else to go. But a sense of contact and closeness felt good after such a long time without it. Zeke made no move against it. "There was always talk about some of the engineers taking it as a challenge to create a genetic body that could physically overpower an android. Even now when the Dante docks, there are a few on standby.

There's always some excuse given for calling a few of them back when a cycle ends. Ridiculous, really."

"Is it?" Zeke looked over at her.

"They have no reason to harm anyone. Even if it weren't forbidden by their programming, it would never make logical sense. They don't do anything without a good reason, and there's no good reason for violence."

Zeke murmured and nestled her head onto the Investigator's shoulder, wrapping an arm around her. The Investigator blinked in slight surprise at the intimacy of the gesture, then gently began to stroke Zeke's hair.

"The most extreme planetary environments," Zeke repeated. "Can you imagine what they've seen? The protectors. The places they've been to? And how long will they keep going? Could they measure time in millions of cycles? Billions? What would any of it mean at that point? Could they witness the collapse of the universe? Could they see the next one born?"

"I think that's giving them a little too much credit."

"What if we've trapped their souls here forever?"

"Their souls?"

"What if we've doomed them? We cursed these children without understanding exactly what it was we were doing. What if we've done the same to these people too? Protectors. Protecting those who cast them into oblivion."

"We have no reason to believe they can't ever be killed," the Investigator said.

"Isn't that the funny thing? Never-ending life would be a curse, wouldn't it? Where is the line? What separates the time from when we seek to avoid death to when we would embrace it?"

"I think there's a middle-ground. A time when we don't fear it, don't run to it, but don't worry so terribly about it."

"Hm, yes," Zeke nodded into the Investigator's shoulder.

"That sounds freeing. I think I live there now. I don't fear it. I only fear the far-flung consequences of decisions made by minds that were never meant to comprehend such measures of time. I'm so afraid for these children." She lifted her head, looking into the Investigator's eyes, and her own were wet with tears. "What will happen to them?" she whispered.

The Investigator could only shake her head. "I don't know."

"Not with this," Zeke dashed her hand over her face. "More than that. What happens after all of it? Where will they go? Oh, we've taken their lives." She collapsed back down onto the Investigator, crying.

"No," the Investigator said, squeezing her tight. "You did none of that. You are here to help. You've done nothing wrong." Zeke's crying quieted after a moment and the two held each other while the sun continued to rise. The Investigator stared out the window at the dim sky. Gently, she kissed the top of Zeke's head. "A day will arrive that I will not live through. It may be in a time and a place so remote from this one that the entire concept of a day is absurd. But a moment will come where I die. I have lived for so long that I do not fear this moment. On the contrary, there are times when I fear that our... unnatural machinations are keeping us trapped in this plane when a more beautiful existence waits for us somewhere beyond. But I'll find out with certainty regardless. What I have learned is that my survival depends very little on the choices I make. As long as I don't steer my craft into an exploding star, I will survive the day. It makes little difference what I do. Each day of my life exists with a degree of safety that is remarkable in human history. I struggled with this existence for a long while after the wars. I could hardly believe my luck that I should be able to live in such security while so many others suffered and had their lives cut short. In all of human existence, the vast majority of us lived such short lives, filled with pain. It seemed so wrong that I should be able to live in peace. But torturing myself about it didn't ensure someone else's happiness. It didn't tip the cosmic scales of the universe. It only made sure that one more person was miserable. My life is a precious gift and I appreciate it whenever it occurs to me, even if I do not understand how it came to be. Everyone deserves that kind of peace, whatever that peace is to them."

Zeke rolled onto her side, looking up at the Investigator. She smiled. "I've never heard you talk so much." The Investigator gave a small laugh. "That sounds like something Tyrick said to me."

"Tyrick?"

"Mm," Zeke nodded. "Peace. Thank you." She took the Investigator's hand and raised it to her lips. "You should go get ready for the day."

"Will you be alright?" The Investigator shook her head. "That was a foolish question."

Zeke smiled softly. "Go on," she whispered.

Geoffrey lay face down on his bed. It was morning. His arm hung off the side and he dragged his hand back and forth along the stone floor. There was a bump where one tile stood just a little higher than its friends. Geoffrey felt his knuckles bump up and over it, again and again, back and forth.

The other students were getting up and going to wash and mumbling to each other. It was very quiet. Everyone was especially quiet around Greta and Stephen.

There was a quick knock at the door and it opened. The students looked in surprise as Professor Arden came into the room. He walked to Geoffrey's bunk. Geoffrey rolled over and sat up, looking confused and tired.

"Geoffrey," said Professor Arden. "You're being transferred. This morning. You and I will be traveling to the jump pad. Collect your things and..." He looked around. "Say goodbye. Meet me in the courtyard as soon as you're ready." He stood and walked out.

Geoffrey sat there. The other students were frozen. What did he feel? He felt nothing. This didn't make any sense. He had almost been killed yesterday. Probably. Transferred? Did that mean expelled? Where was he going? His head hurt. He was coming back though, wasn't he? Wasn't he?

Pency snapped out of it first. "Transferred?" he said. "What the hell does that mean?" He stormed over to Geoffrey's bunk. "What's going on?"

Geoffrey looked up at him, stunned. "I don't know," he stammered. Pency looked angry.

"They can't do this," he said. "You," he stopped. "What if you talk to the Principal? They can't do this," he said firmly.

Stephen ran out of the room.

"Pency?" Geoffrey said, tears building in his eyes. "Are they sending me away?"

"Hey!" Stephen shouted. Professor Arden turned around, startled. "What are you doing?"

"Stephen," started Professor Arden.

"You can't do that!" Stephen shouted. "You can't expel him!"

"Stephen," Professor Arden said again. "He plagiarized a story. He cheated. He copied. He stole the words," Stephen didn't let him finish.

"Bullshit!" Stephen shouted. Professor Arden jerked back in surprise. "That's bullshit!"

"I beg your pardon."

"He didn't copy anything! It was some trick!"

"There was no trick," Professor Arden said, firmly. "And you do not talk to professors that way."

"I'll talk however I damn want," Stephen announced.

"Stephen!"

"Why don't you respect your elders!" Stephen shouted.

"It'll be alright," Pency said. "They can't mean it." He stood awkwardly next to Geoffrey's bed. The other students slowly started to walk closer, fear on their faces. They heard Stephen shouting.

Geoffrey stared at his friend. When would he see him again? Would he see him again? Stephen burst back into the room. He marched to Geoffrey's bed and sat down on the edge of Pency's. "This is bullshit," he said.

"What did Professor Arden say?" asked Lulu.

"I've got detention," said Stephen. "And a bunch of bullshit about plagiarism." Geoffrey winced at the word. Stephen looked at him. "I'm sorry," he said softly. "You're being expelled."

The other children gasped. "Is that what he said?"

Stephen shrugged. "It's what he meant."

Geoffrey slowly got out of bed. He stood, in a fog. There was talking going on around him but he didn't hear it. Pency was close by but he wasn't sure where. His head hurt. It would be okay. He would just pack his things and go. And everything would get sorted out.

He moved mechanically, his mind far away. He had done all of these things before. He had cleared out his locker to organize it and clean it. He had packed all his clothes for a long camping field trip in the rock field. He had taken out his books lots of times, to swap them out with something else. He had done all of these things before. Just never at the same time.

Should he take the books? I guess not. They're the schools' books. And he wasn't a student anymore. Where was he going anyway? Don't think about it. Don't think about it. Think about something else. Folding a habit so it became the bag and packing everything in it. It was a neat trick, wasn't it?

Before he knew it, he was standing with everything he

owned on his back. He looked around the room, finally seeing the other students who were all staring at him. They looked sad. Greta was crying. So was Shinty. Stephen looked angry. Where was Pency? Pency was right next to him. He was looking at the floor. Should he say something? He was being punished. He had plagiarized and now he was being punished. This was right and fair. It had to be. He was wrong. He was the villain.

Geoffrey slowly started to walk toward the door. The students parted but Pency followed him. The two walked through the empty halls. Geoffrey kept looking around, at the walls, the ceiling, the windows, the doors. This was it. This was what he had been afraid of. This was the last time he would see these things. This was the last time he would see Pency.

And then they were standing at the door that led to the courtyard. He stared at Pency. Pency hugged him. Geoffrey's arms lay flat at his sides, pinned by Pency's awkward hug. Geoffrey didn't know what to do or what to say. Shouldn't he say something?

"Well, I..." Geoffrey started, and the words caught in his throat. His chest seized up and tears burst out.

"It's okay," said Pency, looking scared. "It's okay," he repeated. He patted Geoffrey's back. "It's okay."

The two boys stood by the door that would lead Geoffrey out into another life, far away from everything he had known. Geoffrey had stopped crying and was sniffling. Pency didn't know what to do.

Geoffrey opened the door and stepped out.

TWELVE

THE EXIT

Zeke strode up quickly to her quarry, hunched over a large duffel. "Where are you taking him?"

Arden sighed and avoided her eyes. "We'll jump to the station and then transfer back to Central Main. They'll place him."

Zeke stared at his down-turned eyes. He was making a show of checking his bag. "Why are you doing this?"

"You heard the officer," said Arden. "He copied the book and that's it. He can't stay here."

The door opened and Geoffrey walked hesitantly out into the courtyard. He looked confused, bleary. Zeke bit back her anger at Arden and went to the boy, kneeling down in front of him. He looked blankly at her.

"Geoffrey," she said. He nodded. "How are you?"

His eyes were red. "What's happening to me?" he whispered.

Zeke's face squeezed together in pain. "You're..." she started and swallowed back the sob. "You're going to..." she suddenly gasped and stood up, turning away. Geoffrey stared at her back. She walked to Arden. "I'm coming with you. To the jump pad."

"No," said Arden.

"It wasn't a question," said Zeke.

"You'll be gone two days. You don't have a pack. There's no food."

"I'm sure you won't mind sharing," Zeke said evenly.

"Professor," Arden started.

"Don't!" Zeke hissed. "I'll be joining you."

The two stared at each other for a moment while Geoffrey looked on, even more confused and afraid. Arden's eyes narrowed briefly, then he shook his head and turned to the path. "I can't stop you," he said. "Geoffrey," he said, and started walking.

They walked past the outer path and continued on toward the ridge. As they walked, Professor Zeke asked Geoffrey questions. What was he working on now? What did he think about the last book he had read? What were some ideas he might have for characters? Geoffrey tried to answer but he couldn't take his eyes off the ridge line that was getting closer and closer. He was going to go past it. He would finally get to see what lay over the horizon. He just wished Pency was with him.

It seemed like no time at all that they were at the base of the ridge and were walking up the jack-knifing path. Geoffrey kept sneaking glances back to the school as they climbed higher. This was something he had never seen before. In front of him, Arden led, while Zeke was behind him. He kept putting one foot in front of the other, thinking that soon he was going to hit a wall, that there wasn't really anything more, and he had reached the end of the world. But there was no wall and he kept walking, farther and farther from home.

When they reached the top, Professor Arden stopped and allowed him to look out over the landscape. The school lay far away. It looked so small. And the sea was massive, gobbling up the view past the school. Boulders that he knew in perfect detail were like small pebbles and he could barely recognize the places he had spent countless time inhabiting. As he turned around, he saw a vast stretch of land, flat and dead. The horizon seemed so far away, splitting the earth and sky. Geoffrey had never seen so much.

Professor Zeke and Professor Arden both took in the

strange landscape as well. Although not entirely uncommon, it was rare for the professors to go out this far, and it was still a sight they had not gotten used to yet.

"Come on," said Professor Arden, too soon, and began walking down a faint trail.

The Principal walked through the empty student quarters. All of his wards were doing chores. Well, almost all of them. One was walking away from all of it. But he was no longer the Principal's ward, was he? He sighed. What a waste. What a waste of time. What had they been doing here all this time?

A sound caused him to turn and the Investigator entered and nodded once. "We're getting ready to depart," she said. The Principal nodded. "This is..." She paused. "Not as complete a case as I would prefer," she finished, stiffly. "We haven't recovered the book. But..." she shrugged. "That could take an extreme amount of time." The Principal nodded again. "And the murder has taken precedence, so technically our job is done." She waited, but the Principal didn't respond. "I wish things had gone differently."

Now the Principal sighed. "Yes," he said. "I expect I'll be following in all of your footsteps soon enough. A student who plagiarizes. A professor who goes mad and kills another. Not the best record for a Principal. Or a school. Even not considering the scrutiny we find ourselves in." The Investigator looked grim but didn't argue. The Principal was glad for that.

"I'm sorry," the Investigator said.

"Not your fault."

"I'm sorry you didn't get your adventure," she said. The Principal waved his hand, to dismiss it. "This isn't the rote conversation," said the Investigator. The Principal looked up at her now. She stared directly back. "I'm sorry."

His face crumpled and he sat down quickly. The cabinet

was empty, and a small stack of books were on the side table. This was Geoffrey's bunk. This had been Geoffrey's bunk. The Investigator walked to the window and looked out.

"I don't get tired of this view," she said.

The Principal laughed in spite of himself. "That view? Dead rocks and dust?"

"Mm," the Investigator murmured. "I think it's the color." She turned back and walked over to the Principal. "Will you be alright?" she asked.

"Oh, yes, I'll be fine," he said, quickly. "Won't miss the weather here. Just wind, isn't it?"

The Investigator looked at him, sadly. The door opened again and her three officers entered.

"Chief?" said Tyrick. "We're ready to go."

The Investigator nodded at him. She turned back to the Principal. He stared intently at the ground. Sighing, she started to walk away, when it caught her eye.

On Geoffrey's night table was Dracula. He would have copied out his note from this. She picked up the book and flipped through it, marveling again at the pages and pages of words. She thumbed through the middle, then turned to the title page. Bram Stoker. And the copier. And there the date. Not long at all after he had arrived. It would have been one of the very first ones that Professor Lin had done, his handwriting not perfected yet.

Tyrick saw her body twitch from across the room. When she turned to face them, it was as if she had pulled the whole room around her instead of simply rotating herself. Fury was written all across her face.

"Bring me back that man," she whispered. "Arden."

The three officers stared in shock for the briefest moment then vanished out the door.

They had stopped for lunch. Professor Arden was making

a stew over a low fire. Professor Zeke and Geoffrey were playing odds and evens sitting on a rock. The wind had been steady before but now several gusts came pulsating through. They vibrated along the irradiated scrub, letting out a low mournful howl.

"The children of the night," Professor Zeke said.

"What music they make," Geoffrey replied, and she smiled.

"Do you know that was Professor Lin's favorite book?" she said. Her eyes glistened. "He loved it. He was always quoting from it. It was the first book he copied here."

Geoffrey shook his head. "I didn't know that," he said quietly. "I'm very sorry," he said. Professor Zeke tried to laugh away the tears that came. "I think I must have been reading it," said Geoffrey. "I mean, reading his copy. I was reading it. That book, I mean," Geoffrey stopped himself. He didn't know what to say.

Professor Arden came over with two bowls of stew, depositing them on the rock without saying anything, and returning back to the fire.

"He was..." Geoffrey said. "A very good professor. One of our favorites."

Professor Zeke smiled. "He was. Thank you, Geoffrey."

"Did..." Geoffrey started. "Did you love him?"

She smiled again. "Yes, Geoffrey, I did. I loved him. And I love all of you. My good students." Her face was bright. A cloud passed over it suddenly and her eyebrows knitted together. Quickly, she picked up a bowl of stew and took a bite to cover the emotion.

"Geoffrey," Professor Arden said, loudly. The boy turned to look at him. "How did you do it?"

"Arden," Professor Zeke said. "Really."

Professor Arden ignored her. "How about it, Geoffrey? What's the secret?" He was leaning over the stew, stirring.

"I don't..." Geoffrey started to say.

"Come on now," Professor Arden interrupted. "We've been through all that. It's over. There's no harm in telling the truth."

"Ard..." Professor Zeke coughed suddenly. Professor Arden glanced up and then back down at the stew. Professor Zeke held her hand over her mouth and a strange look came over her.

"Geoffrey," Professor Arden called again. Geoffrey was staring at Professor Zeke in fear.

"Is she..." he stopped. "Is she okay?"

"I'm sure she'll be fine," said Professor Arden. "So let's talk."

Professor Zeke leaned back on the rock, her eyes glazing over. Slowly, her arm collapsed from under her and she lay prone. Geoffrey stood up in shock. "What's..." he gasped. "What's happening?"

"What's happening is that you're going to tell me exactly how you copied that story or I'm going to force feed you this." He held up a spoonful of the stew, then dropped it back into the pot.

Geoffrey looked back and forth between Professor Arden and Professor Zeke who was very still. This was all his fault.

"Was there another collection of books? Did Professor Lin have it? Did he tell you about mine? Who else knows about it?"

"What?" whispered Geoffrey.

"The books. Or rather, the book. Carmilla. Where is the extra copy? And who else knows that what we pulled out of the ground yesterday was mine?"

Geoffrey squeezed his eyes shut. Why was it so difficult to process all of this? It was right there in front of him. Why was he frozen? Why was he refusing to accept what was going on? Why was he pretending like he didn't know what was happening to Professor Zeke? It was easier to play dumb. It was easier to let things happen around him. But that had been going on for too long now.

"Geoffrey," said Professor Arden.

Geoffrey picked out a piece of potato from his stew, held it carefully in his hand, and took off running back down the path toward home.

Professor Arden cursed and leapt up, overturning the pot on the fire.

Geoffrey sprinted as fast and as hard as he could. His sandals bounced over the hard path and his habit fluttered behind him. He didn't hear Professor Arden gaining on him, only felt the adult crashing into him, throwing him to the ground. His former teacher knelt over him, fuming, his hands going around Geoffrey's neck.

"Tell me!" he shouted.

Geoffrey reached up and jammed the potato into Arden's face, smearing it across his mouth. Arden jumped backward, rolling on the ground, and wiping at his face. Scrambling to his feet, he spat furiously, scraping the inside of his mouth with his fingers. He never saw Geoffrey with the heavy rock.

The blow exploded on his ankle and he screamed in pain. Spots popped through his vision, and it felt like splinters of bone were stabbing all through his leg. He fell, clutching at his shattered foot. There was the boy, racing off. Arden tried to stand to give chase, and immediately collapsed back into a cloud of dust and agony. Laying in the red dirt, he watched the boy disappear.

Brighton pulled up short and gave a sharp whistle. Third, a short ways ahead, ground to a halt. Brighton knelt down and touched the ground. "Did you feel that?"

"No," said Tyrick, panting.

"The jump pad activated."

"Fuck," said Tyrick.

Third stalked back to them. "What?" he growled.

"Someone jumped," said Brighton.

The three officers stood there for a moment, Brighton and Tyrick catching their breath. "So what?" Third snapped.

Tyrick looked between the two. "He got away."

"We don't know that," said Brighton.

"Yeah," Tyrick sighed. "Come on then."

Third's head snapped around. "Do you hear?" he said. His voice was still guttural. "Someone. The boy." The other two could hear it. A small voice on the wind, reedy and scared, calling for help.

THIRTEEN

THE END

She opened her eyes. She was in her room. Three strands of slow-ivy crept across the ceiling. She sat up, looked around. There was Geoffrey, slumped in her chair, asleep. It was day, but she didn't know the time.

"Geoffrey," she said, quietly. He started awake and stood up quickly.

"Professor Zeke," he said.

"Are you all right?" she asked. He nodded vigorously.

"Yes, I'm fine. And Officer Tyrick fixed you. He said it was the same poison that..." He stopped.

Professor Zeke nodded and closed her eyes. Geoffrey was silent and when she opened her eyes again, she saw tears streaming down his face. "Geoffrey," she said, concerned.

"I'm sorry," he whispered.

"Dear, come here," she held her arms open and he collapsed into them. "It's alright."

He shook his head, his face buried into her shoulder. "I'm sorry," he whispered again.

"It's alright," she insisted.

"It was my fault," he said.

"What was your fault?"

"Professor Lin."

"What?"

"It was because I copied from his book and Professor Arden recognized it and thought that I had, that he had done it, that Professor Lin had done it, and it was my note but he thought it wasn't," Geoffrey was sobbing. "And it wouldn't even have happened if I hadn't written that story. It was my fault!"

Professor Zeke blinked in surprise at the onslaught of information and the crying child in her arms. "Geoffrey," she said. "That wasn't your fault. You didn't cause any of this."

"Yes I did!" he shouted. "I was part of it. If it hadn't been for me, it wouldn't have happened. Or if I had just done things a little differently, it wouldn't have happened." He sobbed again. "He wouldn't have..." he broke down.

"But it wasn't your fault," Professor Zeke said. "You didn't mean any harm."

"It doesn't matter," Geoffrey said, still crying. "I did it."

"But..." Professor Zeke started.

"Would the same thing have happened if it had been someone else?" demanded Geoffrey. "It would have been different. They would have written a different story, done things differently, just enough so that none of this would have happened. It was because of me."

Professor Zeke stopped. Geoffrey continued to cry. It was such an unlikely collection of events, all strung together, all leading to their terrible conclusion. A tenuous chain made of rings as delicate as soap bubbles. The smallest change would have led to drastically different results.

"Geoffrey," Professor Zeke said. He continued to cry. "Geoffrey," she said firmly. She took his shoulders and held him back. He sniffled and looked at the ground. "Geoffrey," she said again, giving him a small shake. He looked up, his face miserable. "I don't care," she said. "I don't care." He looked at her, confused. "I don't care about whatever effect you caused here. Do you hear me?" He nodded slowly, still confused. "I don't care," she repeated, emphatically.

"But," Geoffrey started to cry again. "It's because of me that Professor Lin is gone."

"I don't care," she said again. "I still love you. I still accept you."

The small boy fell again, crying.

"So what really happened?" asked the Principal.

The three officers looked to the Investigator, who was sitting at the table in the faculty conference room now. Tyrick was reminded of the contrast to the last time when they sat in this room and she had stood staring out the window.

"Let's wait a moment," the Investigator said. "I've asked a few more to join us."

The Principal sat back in his chair. It had felt like he had been doing nothing but running around, either physically or mentally, for days. Just taking a moment to pause felt strange. It felt like he was forgetting to do something important. The door opened and Professor Nalin entered. The Principal looked expectantly at the Investigator. She nodded to Nalin but stayed silent.

After another few minutes the door opened again and Professor Zeke and Geoffrey entered. The Investigator gestured for them to sit. Geoffrey was holding Zeke's hand and didn't seem like he would ever let go.

After some shuffling around, everyone was settled. The Investigator looked around the table. "Geoffrey," she said softly, looking directly at him. "We're going to be talking about the investigation. I wanted you to be here so you could hear it directly. Some of this might be difficult for you to hear but I think it's important. And you don't have to say anything. You're not under investigation anymore." Geoffrey's eyes widened but he nodded silently. The Investigator glanced at the professors and the officers. "This is not strictly according to protocol," she said.

Tyrick bit his lip and the Principal looked at her intently, but neither spoke.

"Professor Nalin?" she said. Nalin looked up. "Were you able to complete your scan?"

"Yes," she said. "I modified the scan to check for a wider

range of chemical signatures." She paused. "It was able to detect the traces of the hidden cache that we found. That Geoffrey found." She paused again. "But there was nothing else out there. Of the books themselves, they were almost certainly Professor Arden's. Bol Win had handled them at least once prior to the..." She searched for a word. "Incident," she settled on. "With Geoffrey. But the most common genetic footprint was Arden."

The Investigator nodded. She took a breath. "Professor Arden killed Professor Lin," she said. She paused, not for dramatic effect, but to collect her thoughts. The others waited patiently. "The note that Greta slipped under bol Win's door? The one Geoffrey had copied from the book he was reading. Dracula. It had been copied by Professor Lin. Bol Win showed the note to Arden, and Arden, the handwriting expert, recognized that it was Lin. Arden thought that Lin had slipped the note under bol Win's door, that Lin knew about the secret cache of books in the rocks. The cache that was Arden's all along. So he poisoned Lin. The same poison that he used on Professor Zeke. When he learned of his error later on, that it had really been Geoffrey who had written the note, he assumed Geoffrey knew about the books. So he needed to kill him too."

Geoffrey winced at this. Zeke squeezed his hand a little tighter.

"How?" asked Professor Nalin. "How did he have a poison that could do that?"

"Time and a morbid curiosity. He followed military updates quite closely. We need to do a closer search for compounds, but we'll get more information once we have a conversation with him in person."

"How did bol Win know about Arden's books?" asked the Principal. "He had found it in the desert when Geoffrey came across him."

The Investigator shrugged. "He's been here longer than anyone apart from you, and he spent more time with the faculty. He'd probably known about it for cycles. I doubt Arden was as clever as he imagined when it came to keeping a secret. What bol Win didn't know, and neither did Lin, was how Geoffrey had managed to copy Carmilla when it wasn't in the cache of books. Arden must have thought another professor had a secret collection. If he had one, why not someone else?"

"So who had this other secret collection?"

"There isn't one," the Investigator said.

"How did Geoffrey copy Carmilla then?"

Geoffrey gritted his teeth.

The Investigator tucked her head down. "He didn't," she said. The whole room stared at her. "Bol Win was the closest."

Third raised his eyebrows. "Are we dead then?"

The Investigator laughed softly. "No, as it turns out. But..." She paused, and looked at the Principal. "It was just chance."

The Principal looked flustered. "That's not possible," he said.

"You can't rule out other explanations," said Nalin. She gestured helplessly. "Some kind of..." She struggled for words. "Inspiration from an unknown source. Something. Just chance? That's not possible," she echoed the Principal.

She nodded slowly. "It is possible. It's just very unlikely. But it was just a collection of decisions that happened, by chance, to fall perfectly in line with one another. Each word just so happened to be the same choice that someone else made long ago. One person thought of it, so why not another?"

"But..." said the Principal. "The sheer amount of randomness in picking one word over another." He was gasping at the idea. "Every bit of punctuation?"

The Investigator nodded. "That kind of randomness is not something that we like to accept. So we tried to construct our own stories around it, our own explanations. Something, anything to explain away this bizarre turn of events. Some way he had read a copy, or some way that his mind was controlled or affected. Some reason. But we were just grasping at noise." She stared at her hands. "There was no reason. No grand design. All we did was chase our tails," she finished softly, thinking on the repercussions.

Geoffrey had listened in a state of shock. The Investigator was saying that it wasn't his fault. For the first time, someone had believed him. He hadn't copied anything. But he knew there had to be a reason for it, for why he had managed to recreate this story word for word. What the Investigator was saying didn't make sense. No reason? Just chance? That's not how things were supposed to happen. There was always something. In everything he read, there was always a meaning behind the events. So wasn't that supposed to be how real life was like? Shouldn't there be something to uncover?

His hand had fallen from Zeke's. He sat in disbelief. The Principal and Professor Nalin were still arguing. But the Investigator never wavered. He wasn't going to be expelled. He wasn't going to be an outcast. But after everything that had happened, he still didn't have an answer.

The boy and the Investigator stood in the courtyard. Geoffrey was tugging at the sleeves of his habit, frowning at the ground, unsure of what to say. It still didn't seem possible that all the troubles were behind him now. That he wasn't getting expelled or punished even, that he would travel far beyond the school. He knew the Investigator was responsible but he didn't know what to say to her.

The Investigator looked down at the small child in front of her, a boy who had lived so much longer than her and who had seen so much less of the universe. She squatted down onto her heels so she could look up into his eyes, and took his hands.

"Geoffrey," she said. His nervous face turned to her. "Thank you for help with my investigation." His confusion seemed to deepen.

"But I didn't..."

"You did," she said, squeezing his hands. "You did. Thank you. But I have one more favor to ask of you."

"A favor?"

The Investigator nodded. "Keep writing. Your teacher tells me you've taken a little break. I know that you might be a little cautious right now, but there's no need for that. If you want to write, do so. Don't be afraid. Can you do that for me?"

He nodded slowly.

"Thank you." She gave his hands one last squeeze and stood up. "Take care of yourself."

Geoffrey looked out across the dust and rocks. "You're leaving?" She nodded. Something occurred to him. "Oh, okay." Now he was rocking back and forth on his feet, anxious. "I have to go." And he was off like a shot back toward the school, shouting over his shoulder. "See you later!"

He ran past the Principal making his way toward the Investigator. She waited for him to arrive, shaking his head.

"Just by chance," said the Principal. The Investigator smiled. "Chance."

"You don't believe it?"

The Principal sighed. "Is that what you honestly think happened?" The Investigator shrugged. "What if..." the Principal looked up at the sky. "What if he saw the story as a child, even before the treatment. And it got lodged in his memory somehow. Couldn't that happen? Or maybe before he came here? He saw it somehow."

The Investigator snorted a laugh. "Were there any books where he came from?" she asked, turning to look at The Principal.

He turned his face to the ground. "No," he said softly. "But there has to be something. There has to be a reason," he insisted, almost to himself. "For all of this."

"You don't like questions where the answer is already known," said the Investigator, kindly. "This is your lucky day." The Principal looked up at her. She smiled, sadly. "This is a question that has no answer. And it never will." She took a deep breath and turned to look out across the sea. "Maybe he saw it long ago. Maybe he was touched by the hand of gods. Maybe he is the latest reincarnation of a long line of poets and authors. Maybe he was possessed. It doesn't matter." She turned to look at The Principal again. "It doesn't matter," she repeated. "We will never know. The boy didn't cheat. His actions were blameless and there is no harm to either his integrity or to your school." The Principal blinked at the formalness of her speech. "My report will say that it was chance and that is the end of it. It's as good an answer as any."

He felt tears coming into his eyes. "But my friends," he said, so softly. "Two dead and another a fugitive. For this? For nothing?"

She reached out and took his shoulder. "I am so sorry," she said. "They died..." She took a deep breath. "They died because of our own foolishness. They died because we needed an answer so badly. Because we can't stand to look out into the void and see nothing but chaos."

The Principal reached a hand up to press against hers on his shoulder. They stood together for a long moment. The Principal closed his eyes and imagined floating up above them and looking down on the two figures standing there. Then floating up higher and higher, seeing them get smaller, fade into nothing, the school fade as well, everything getting farther and farther away, smaller and smaller. He took a deep breath and opened his eyes, looking out at the boulders, the ridge, the blue sky, the sea. "What do you think happened?" he said again. "Do you think it was chance?"

The Investigator patted his shoulder once and removed her hand. She looked straight into him. "What are the odds that the two of us would be standing here right now?" she asked. "Think about your life, every decision that led to another. Every choice, every random encounter, every conscious action. The roads not taken, the doors not opened. Each one that would have led you down a completely different path. Now imagine that for your parents. And their parents. And so on. And multiply everything by two to account for the person standing next to you right now. Go back even further. The evolution of life, the formation of this planet. A few million miles difference from Sol and we're never here. In all the history of your life, mine, of humanity, and of the universe itself, what are the odds that the two of us would be standing here in this moment?"

The Principal laughed softly. "Incalculable," he said.

The Investigator nodded. "Which is more likely? That a story once told could be told again or that we two might be here?"

"Hm," the Principal grunted, nodded. "I guess that makes me lucky," he said.

Now it was the Investigator's turn to grunt. "I don't see that. A little different roll of the dice and this whole mess might have been avoided. I'm pleased to have met you," she said. "But I think we'd be better off being strangers and still having your friends with you."

The Principal nodded. "If none of this had happened, then today would be like the countless ones that came before. And so would tomorrow. But I won't let that happen. We're going to continue with my plan. We're going to travel the stars."

"Are you sure?" asked the Investigator. "It could be dangerous. You could lose more friends."

He nodded slowly. "A ship is safest in the harbor," he said. "But that is not what ships are built for."

"I like that quote," said the Investigator. "Where does it come from?"

"No idea," the Principal said. "I've completely forgotten." The two laughed.

"Well," the Investigator said, feeling her throat tighten. "We will be on our way. The Erinyes will be after Arden and I need to file my report."

"Will they find him?"

"They have never failed and they aren't about to start now." The Principal nodded. "Thank you for your hospitality," the Investigator said. "I don't suppose we will run into each other again."

"Ah," the Principal shrugged. "What are the odds?" He smiled and opened his arms, and the Investigator returned the embrace. "Now," he said gruffly, standing back. "I believe you have one more goodbye to make." He walked back into the school, past Zeke who was standing in the doorway.

The Investigator waited as Zeke walked slowly toward her. She wished that the time wouldn't move so quickly. She wished that this moment wouldn't become lost in her memory a thousand years from now. She wished that she could hold on to the look in Zeke's eyes forever.

"Hello," said Zeke.

"Hello." The Investigator felt small and broken, standing there.

"Thank you for finding out what happened to Lin," Zeke said. The Investigator nodded. "Thank you for being here." She stepped forward, putting her arms around the Investigator. "Thank you," she whispered.

The Investigator held on tightly, her eyes squeezed shut. Remember this moment. Please. If nothing else, just this one moment. It didn't happen to someone else. Not some child that you don't even recognize anymore. Not a stranger. It happened to you and it exists forever. She opened her eyes and stepped back, holding Zeke in her eyes instead of her arms. "Will you go to the stars?"

Zeke's eyes shone brightly as she nodded. "I wouldn't miss it for anything."

The three officers exited the school, carrying their packs. With a gentle squeeze of Zeke's hand, the Investigator smiled once and turned to go. Zeke watched them walk out into the dusty red, watched them get smaller next to rocks that never seemed to change size, watched them disappear. She sighed, looked up at the sky, to the hidden worlds that she would soon visit, and went back into the school.

From the roof, Geoffrey stared at the ridge line, waiting. At last, he saw it. The four figures, just a blur at this distance, but the line was broken, if only for a few seconds.

The school sat by the edge of a sea. It had stood there for a long time. I wish I could tell you how long.

About the Author

Davin Hall is a former data analyst and cartographer. They spent ten years working in policing before resigning in 2020. They live in Greensboro, North Carolina and when not writing, they can usually be found working at a high ropes course surrounded by lemurs and tigers.

CPSIA information can be obtained
at www.ICGtesting.com
Printed in the USA
LVHW102237120822
725867LV00003B/82